PRAISE FOR

"Martin Ott's *Shadow Dance* is the perfect L.A. Noir novel for our times, with a little of everything—romance, drugs, film-making, PTSD, twisted families, repressed memories, and mysterious disappearances—all set in a sketchy strip club in Little Persia on L.A.'s West Side. Ott's Buddy Rivet is a deeply flawed character, a hard-luck Army vet, who readers will root for, a soulful guy who wants to save the world but isn't sure he can save himself. This book is *L.A. Confidential* meets *The Family Fang*, with all the deception and double-cross of a terrific crime story, told in breathless, blunt-force-trauma prose."

— Clifford Garstang, author of *Oliver's Travels* and *The Shaman of Turtle Valley*

"*Shadow Dance* is a powerful dance of language, a shadow of history, military trauma, and a unique coming-of-age tale of a man's own past and attempt to move forward. Martin Ott has created yet another masterpiece full of suspense, beauty, and heart. This book is chilling, wonderful, a must."

— Kim Chinquee, author of *Snowdog*

"Strange how the language of relationships can mimic that of war." That's Buddy, a/k/a West, leading this *Shadow Dance* like a spastic Astaire, and his musings go to the heart of Martin Ott's imagining. A novel smeared by the torture in the Middle East, this Dance amounts finally to a twisted but miraculous cleansing, a rediscovery of love, by way of an eye-popping and wisecracking tour of the L.A. underworld. You've never had such fun at an exorcism. Martin Ott has created yet another masterpiece full of suspense, beauty, and heart. This book is chilling, wonderful, a must."

- John Domini, author of *The Color Inside a Melon*

"With crisp, gimlet-eyed storytelling, Martin Ott's *Shadow Dance* dramatizes compellingly the tough truth that, whether you're enlisted in Afghanistan, home in Louisiana, or trying to do right in Los Angeles, war never ends."

- Mark Wish, author of *Watch Me Go*, founding editor of *Coolest American Stories*

"'Something bad's going to happen,' one *Shadow Dance* character remarks to West, a man who picked up his name on the run, heading west. The protagonist wonders how he knows. 'Because something bad is always going to happen.' And there you have it, the noir credo perfectly expressed, the central understanding in every dark thriller or hardboiled tale of the streets, and my oh my, does it express the tenor of our age. But among literature's—and pulp fiction's—empyrean of unforgettable tough guys, Martin Ott's fascinating protagonist breaks the mold—a tormented, introspective empath and reader of Travis McGee detective stories tough guy.… Martin Ott's prose weaves mood, velocity, grit and occasional concentrations of poetry. 'Outside, the long day burned as though a distant fire was burning up the bowl of America.' *Shadow Dance* joins the great tradition of novels that investigate dark corners within the light-filled city."

- Suzanne Lummis, author of *Open 24 Hours*, Blue Lynx Poetry prize winner, host and creator of poetry.la's *They Write by Night*, a YouTube series exploring the connection between poetry and film noir.

"Ott's prose crackles and sizzles. There's never a dull moment, right to the riveting end. It's the kind of novel Hemingway might have written had he been alive today."

- Erik Martiny, author of *Night of the Long Goodbyes*

SHADOW DANCE

07/12/23

Martin Ott

Regal House Publishing

Published by
Regal House Publishing, LLC
Raleigh, NC 27605
All rights reserved

ISBN -13 (paperback): 9781646033799
ISBN -13 (epub): 9781646033805
Library of Congress Control Number: 2022949229

Cover images and design by © C. B. Royal

Regal House Publishing, LLC
https://regalhousepublishing.com

Printed in the United States of America

Dedicated to everyone I served with in the military

"Time flies over us but leaves its shadow behind."

—Nathaniel Hawthorne

1

SHADOW IN LIMBO

You're not invisible. You may think you've snuck away, dropped off the grid, kept it all on the down-low. Don't fool yourself, though. You've left a ripple of your presence wiggling in the intersection of darkness and light like a villain's gloved fingers. Sometimes people squint at you as you dart along the periphery. Whether you try to do the wrong thing or the right thing, you ping along the moral axis of yesterdays and tomorrows. Up until now, I'd always counted myself with more *rights* than *wrongs*. And like everyone, I was followed by a shadow. Mine was barely the size of dog. At first, I thought it was Pops who spun tall tales with a fluency not unlike a second language. Later, I kidded myself that it was women looking to bed me, the ones I tried to ignore. But it was something else, a fleeting passenger that hounded me as a boy and haunted me as a man.

I joined the army the day I turned eighteen and ordered the shadow to stay home. Strangely, it listened for a time, losing itself in the sunset on the bayou, a dull fire shimmering in the eyes of everyone I left behind. There was no family to see me off (a story for another day) and my girlfriend Deirdre had told me I was a *fucking idiot*. Not that I blamed her for calling it like she saw it. Suffice to say that Private Buddy Rivet was looking to reinvent himself, and had to get himself sent to a damn war in the process. No one ever told me that I had a lick of sense. Especially not my best friend Solomon St. James, one of my fellow latchkey kids whose parents had jobs on the gambling riverboat *Aces*.

Unlike Deirdre, he didn't think I was an asshat for not emailing while I was in Kabul. He knew I was intentionally difficult. Solomon mailed me letters from a string of small towns as he drifted from Lake Charles. He'd followed a progression of women westward, finding gigs as a DJ, enjoying his time on the road. I went the other direction. After spending so much time skirting the law in the company of my hoodlum parents and hoodlum friends, I needed order. I found it at a deserted Soviet base in Afghanistan—Bagram Airfield. My role there as military police was an impossible job. How do you help interrogators stop a war in a place where conflict is the same as the sun rising and falling? It made me hate...well...everyone.

The ghosts in my past were quieted by the ghosts from the airbase. I paced my rounds in the spaces between sunset and sunrise. I became scary in my own right, like the ferryman on the River Styx. But there were no coins passed to me, no price for passage into the darkness. Anyone I transported to and from the interrogation rooms was doomed and they knew it. We all looked away when the sun went down, blinded by our fears.

Now I was back in purgatory in a floating gas station in the middle of the Atlantic Ocean. This was probably not a fair assessment of Terceira Island, one of nine in the Azores, where the US kept an Air Force base called Lajes Field. For nearly sixty years soldiers passed through here to missions all over the world, some known, others hush-hush. As the troops in Afghanistan cycled out, the usage of Lajes Field was on the decline, at least until the US invested in another war. Our C-17 transport plane was undergoing minor repairs after a trip from Manas, which had passed through Iceland. Jet lag didn't even begin to cover my feeling of being out of time and place.

We'd been set up with temporary shelter for the night in an open-room barracks. It was like a five-star hotel after becoming used to cots and rough living. Used to explosions and broken sleep. Used to having a rifle within arm's reach the way a mother sleeps next to her baby. It would be my first mattress in more than a year. I couldn't sleep, though. And neither could my squad of MPs. We tried playing cards in the mid-afternoon sun boring through our windows but somehow all of us were grumpy about the shifting fortunes in our hands. We ended up trading dollars for Euros with a couple of off-duty airmen in the mostly empty lounge, changed clothes, and wandered off base toward the signs for the nearest town. It was our first chance to stretch our legs after nearly a full day of flying.

We marched single file with me trailing in the rear. Staff Sergeant Lasicky was on point, and I made it a point to steer clear of him. The other MPs hated him as well, but he kept them all close in the way of a 1950s father, all commands and insults. Lasicky was a piece of work. In the space of a couple of hours, he made our squad feel guilty enough to go along for this unauthorized trip, while also making it clear that anyone getting out of line could be punished. This was next-level manipulation from a military police officer used to operating in the shadows. The guys were filled with bravado as the sun lowered on our shoulders, telling each other which woman was going to get the business when they got back to Louisiana.

"Rivet's boyfriend is going to be jealous when he gets back after all the sweet loving he gave those prisoners."

"Jackass," I muttered under my breath every tenth step, counting to keep my cool, counting to keep myself from beating him within an inch of his life. The closer I came to landing in the states, something feral was stirred in me, perhaps the reason I'd avoided leave during my tours. A voice inside of me whispered to turn back, but the story of my life was never turning back. I didn't want to be blinded by what might be there.

The countryside quickly gave way to a packed seaside town of white houses with tan roofs. We soon found ourselves on narrow streets with wave patterns on the sidewalks matching the designs on white gates dividing intersections. The sea calligraphy felt like runes, protection against primal forces. I wondered if this included the US military.

We ended up on *Rua de Jesus* and ducked into one of the cafés. The establishment had no name but featured an image above the door of a pig in a chef's hat on its two hind legs holding a beer and winking toward the sidewalk. Plastic tables and chairs had been set out beneath temporary awnings flapping in the salty breeze wafting from the ocean. A few other servicemen from the base were already drinking there. The locals, meanwhile, congregated inside at long wooden tables. A division existed between the islanders and soldiers in this Azores crossroads situated somewhere between Portugal, the United States, and sleepy paradise.

During orientation, we'd been warned that we couldn't wear uniforms outside Lajes Field. We were all dressed in army-issue brown T-shirts and jeans, still a gang even without the camouflage. I separated myself from the rest of the guys and sat at a small table pushed against one of the open glass doors. I was past worrying what the other MPs thought about me. I wouldn't be pals with any of those fuckers after we returned to civilian life. I was the *stickler* for following rules, the *tattletale* for raising concerns to the company commander, the *weirdo* who liked spending time by myself. My closest friends had been the prisoners and, of course, my books, all of which had been left behind.

Now the only reading material I had was the most recent letter from Solomon. I'd looked at it enough on my final days that the folds were starting to fray. Not unlike our equipment. Our clothing. Our sense of humor. The other ex-prison guards started chugging beer at a table near the entrance, loud and getting louder. I tried not to listen to them from my table straddling worlds. Solomon's cursive was still childish, with lavish hooks and swoops. Yet there was a section of the letter I kept coming back to, a sign that everything wasn't okay: *I'm banging this married chick and she's messing with my mind. Her husband is my boss's brother and I'm in way too deep with this family. They're into some strange-ass shit. I can't quit her or my job here at Club Paradise. I'm thinking about bolting but the set-up's sweet. Too bad you aren't here to set me straight.*

Yes, I'd always been there for him. Even on the evening he decided to make a visit to our math teacher Mrs. Jenkins. The guys my age called her Mrs. Jerkins for how many of them incorporated her into their whack-off fantasies. Solomon, as usual, had a straightforward plan to hook up with her. He knew that her husband was drinking at Catfish Bar watching Monday Night Football and he decided to see if there was anything behind her in-class flirtations. After the sun fell, we pedaled our bikes over to her house in a subdivision adjacent to the school. I stood watch while he went inside with a thin cover story of needing help with his math homework. Once he was in the door, he figured things would take care of themselves.

Solomon had an impressive record with girls our own age. I still found it surprising, though, when our sexy math teacher invited him inside and closed the door behind him. I was supposed to signal him if someone *came a knockin'* with a referee's whistle we'd stolen from her husband, our gym teacher Bad-eye Jenkins. The dude's nickname came from a glass eye he liked to pluck from his right socket and point at you when he was pissed. Which was most of the time. No one knew what had caused the injury. Some say it was a hunting accident. Others a high school football injury. Still others believed he pulled it out himself after the Saints lost one too many games on the final drive. Regardless, it made the hulk of a man in a tracksuit seem more monster than human.

What came next was partially my fault. I was spacing out behind a tree and didn't notice the pickup truck barreling down the two-lane road with a single headlight—like truck like owner. I clinched the whistle in my lips and froze. Bad-eye had the window down and would hear that something was up, would be in the driveway in moments. I launched myself, pedaling furiously onto the shoulder of the road, catching the truck turning into the driveway.

Too fast, I remember myself thinking before I got clipped and the world grew fuzzy. That night I got my first concussion, several dislocated fingers, and road rash from sliding across the hood and onto the asphalt. My arms kept me from breaking my neck, I suppose. The ambulance ride was kind of cool, even though my folks had to move to dodge paying the bill. Most importantly, Solomon had a chance to get away from the scene. In the emergency room and for weeks after, I felt like a badass.

I stared at the last two fingers of my left hand, still curved from the dislocation, clutching Solomon's letter. I'd always found comfort and meaning in scars the way others looked at tattoos. Each of them defined me in some way.

"Walk away, witch!" Lasicky belted out from across the courtyard.

Some weird shit was going down. A thin woman in white shorts, a black sweater, and purple headscarf backed away from the table of MPs, speaking softly but quickly as though throwing a curse. She wasn't moving quickly enough for Lasicky. He tossed a half glass of beer at her face and she raced for my table. I grabbed her hand in passing and stood up, wiping her dripping face with the tail of my shirt.

I glanced over at the bar but the waiters weren't coming outside. Lasicky challenged me with a stare. He wanted me to throw down. "Waste of a good beer," he muttered. The woman looked at me as though I was a scientific curiosity, her scowl transforming into a smile. My free hand unclenched from a fist and she held that one as well.

"I'm sorry about my friends," I said.

"Are they really your friends?" she asked in Portuguese accent.

"No, guess not."

"Then don't apologize."

"Maybe Rivet isn't a fag after all," Lasicky called out. "Maybe he just likes old hags."

I turned sideways so I wouldn't see his smug grin. "Why did that idiot get mad at you?" I asked.

"I read his palm and told him the truth. That he was going to be seriously injured. And soon. He told me he didn't survive a war only to have some bitch put a hex on him."

The boys from my unit were all Louisiana born and bred, with a healthy dislike for anything that smacked of black magic.

"I'm already cursed. Try me," I suggested.

The woman sighed as though she didn't want to discuss the future with someone she liked. She opened my right palm and stared at it for what seemed an eternity. A jagged scar cut across it from the truck accident where the bike's handbrake had sliced deep into my flexor tendon. The injury had left a blank spot in the middle of my palm, where the lines disappeared.

"Your childhood is misery."

"That much I know," I said.

"Your love and fate line intersect in the future. You will face decisions that could hurt you or the people you love. I can't help you with advice. You're living in that blank spot, that dead zone."

Her voice unnerved me and I felt drunk even though I'd only sipped on my beer. *Dead zone* felt exactly right for the past few years of my life. I emptied out my pocket and shoved my remaining Euros in her hands, asking, "What choice should I make?"

"You can't save everyone. When the time comes, save yourself."

The woman pocketed the money and slipped out the side entrance. I ignored the jeers from Lasicky and headed inside to use the bathroom. No wonder the locals gave us a wide berth outside. We were returning to America with violence boiling in our blood, which no amount of beer would be able to thin out or wash away. We would be rejoining our country soon as security guards or police officers with the belief that we had the right to inflict the pain we felt inside. We would be ghost soldiers for years to come, unable or unwilling to admit that the battle raged within us.

Inside the toilet, I ran my hands under the faucet as though it could change the story in my palms, change the story of a past that had carried me half a world away. I breathed in the scent of stale beer and urine, and stared at my reflection in the mirror. The fluorescents flickered above and a small figure darted out the door, perhaps some child returning to parents or else a trick of the light. Brown eyes, thin face, long pale neck, and extended chin were framed in the looking glass, the telltale signs of my French ancestry. And something else as well. The source of the Rivet family curse, the slave in our family history who'd bourn a male child pale enough to pass himself off as white. The mother who cursed her own flesh and blood in order to get revenge.

Pops was a man who liked whispering about secrets and kept a few of his own. He lied for profit and lied for laughs. When it came to the family curse, though, he was sober. According to him, our deeds made us pay for the past and the present. Moms thought that our belief in the curse was a self-fulfilling prophecy. Many of us in the South had shadows that hid behind their men. It was impossible to be an American without standing on shoulders, standing on bones. We were blind in the darkness and the light. *Save yourself.* Good advice from the palm reader. Tough to save what you didn't understand.

Then something dawned on me. A vision as clear as any memory. In it, I saw how Lasicky would get what was coming to him. In it, I saw how my life was going to change.

2

Shadow in Motion

Click clack. Tick tock. The cab's tires spun on the highway. I stared out at the passing trees and buildings, my eyes unfocused until the buildings and trees morphed into shapeless forms that could be anything or anyone. I'd always been in motion, either on *Aces* for summer trips in my parents' cabin or in our yearly migration with the other riverboat families to ramshackle apartments. The ancient cab coughed and clacked over potholes on the winding Louisiana country road. The cabbie and I were both disasters in motion, him for ignoring the age of Uber and me for trying to escape the inevitable. Fate had brought us together in our shared desperation. Why else would he agree to transport a dude with bloody knuckles?

We hadn't spoken to each other since he pocketed the two hundred bucks-upfront fair to haul my ass all the way from Barksdale Air Force Base to the outskirts of Lake Charles. The back of the cabbie's head was bald, crinkly, and pale like a pulled-out ditch weed. The geezer hummed in a thick accent, Ukrainian or Polish, or maybe even Russian. For some reason, he couldn't quite avoid the divots on the road. Hell, for all I knew he aimed at them to provide a bass to his tuneless accompaniment of a country song warning men about the dangers of women, fistfights, and rifles. If only I'd heard this sooner.

Perhaps I scared him. God knows, I scared myself with thoughts as bleak as the oil-soaked waterways spooling by on the small bridges we were passing. Outside, the flat damp terrain seemed foreign after a year living a mile above sea level in the hills of Kabul. We would soon be arriving at a place I'd never been but now called home, Perdido Park. Lost Park. The place I'd parked my girlfriend. I'd have to tell her soon why I'd been an idiot. Again.

My tours to Afghanistan had messed up my relationship with Deirdre and the past couple of years of our engagement to be engaged. The problems should have been obvious: my age, her age, my inexperience with women, her need to write letters because I refused to email, text, or own any "smart" device, my money now her money. She was lonely. That much was clear from her recent admission that her best friend was my uncle Miles. He was a con man who'd parlayed a nasty spill off the back porch of a nightclub into a lawsuit that left him with just enough scratch to party at night, sleep during the day, and tomcat around with a progressively younger line of girlfriends.

Moms would have asked me how I'd managed three tours in Afghanistan without getting a scratch on me only to have things blow up the moment I came home. Pops would have slapped me upside the head for joining the army in the first place, before trying to get me drunk. Neither of my folks would have understood how their absence unraveled everything. I started believing in the curse. I stopped believing in myself. I started believing I could do some good in a muddy conflict even as it was winding down. Becoming an MP made me believe I could bring some order to the chaos. Guarding POWs suited my temperament. We stuffed way too many people in boxes, home and abroad.

This sometimes meant ignoring the orders of asshole interrogators who asked us to place prisoners in stress positions. The psychology was to make them feel responsible for their own pain. There were also nights when the temperatures dipped and the blankets had holes. The nights of bad music played too loud. The nights when the prisoners lost hope, prayed, and cried like kids.

Some MPs, like Lasicky, went along with the program. They were the ones used by the OGA (Other Government Agency), slang for the CIA. Those douchebags showed up at the ancient Soviet airbase with hipster beards and dressed in civvies.

They did not follow our protocol or share their missions. They showed me nearly as much hatred as the prisoners they put through the paces. They acted as if the Geneva Convention did not apply to them. This arrogance brushed off on the army interrogators and other MPs on my team. Even though the conflict in Afghanistan was coming to a close, it didn't stop the worst of the men from acting like the worst of men.

My military police unit had spent the past few months transitioning the Bagram Internment Facility back to the Kabul government. We were finally heading home to be reassigned to Fort Polk. The war for us was ending. That hadn't stopped me from turning my homecoming into a battlefield. My tour of duty was up, except for the paperwork, and my dumbass decision on the airfield would land my ass in Leavenworth. Imagine being stuffed in a cramped cell after already spending years as a jailer. I couldn't take the thought of being under lock and key. No thanks.

That wasn't to say Lasicky didn't deserve the punch that likely broke his nose. When he blew me kisses on the airfield and told me how he'd placed one of our stool pigeons back into the general populations to get beaten by the other prisoners, I lost my shit. Should I have taken my complaint up to my chain of command? Probably. When I told him the prisoner's name was *Niles*, he'd laughed and called me a *terrorist lover*.

No use sniveling about what came next. Consequences for tagging sarge loomed in the bake of an unnaturally hot Louisiana summer afternoon. I missed my trusty aviator sunglasses, now crushed beneath the boots of squad members who'd pulled me off Lasicky. Outside, the sun was too bright, a torture device. Was I being overly dramatic? Maybe. But I'd just spent the past year guarding prisoners on the night shift and embracing the life of a military vampire. I'd existed in the shadows pooling from tagging, bagging, and dragging POWs. My day senses now sucked and more poorly made decisions seemed inevitable.

A bullet-ridden highway marker whizzed past. We were on Country Road 387, Big Lane Road, cutting south from the potbelly of Lake Charles. The filthy lake of my hometown was shaped like a stomach. It had rivulets above and below, like a spindly esophagus and intestines leading to the crapper of Old Man River. The palm reader had warned me about the dead zone in the heart of my palm. Louisiana was the dead zone of America. So much had been rubbed out in my life here by the friction of family and the dark river water pouring through our veins.

"Do you believe in curses?" I asked.

"Yup, I'm driving you," the cabbie said. "This trip isn't going to be worth the money."

"At least gas prices are better," I said.

"Better than what? A hole in the head?"

"Suppose so."

"Don't matter. I've got no fare back to Shreveport on the return trip."

"We all make mistakes," I said.

"I guess your parents would know something about that."

The cabbie's delivery was deadpan. He was either a cold-hearted SOB or king of the local comedy club. I was started to get the feeling that I'd underestimated him.

"Do you have kids?" I asked him.

"I know that joy and misery."

"Do you think we should be held accountable for the mistakes of our parents?"

"Definitely," the cabbie said, his voice rising above the staticky radio like a preacher. "The sins of the father are visited upon the son."

"You make Christianity sound like a curse."

"The Arabs sure think so," he said, ripping a magnificent belch that carried past the windshield, beyond the ozone, past the space-time continuum. Radio waves were carried along with it, silencing the speakers, softening the spin of bald tires, leaving us in a relative state of silence.

"My family's last name is Rivet," I said, clearing my throat.

Just like that the spell was broken, and the sounds of the car and road returned.

"My gym teacher in high school was a Rivet. We used to call him Old Man Rivet because he spent his spare time on the river fishing and avoiding his old lady."

"In French, it means to hold things together, but in my family everything is always falling apart."

"Jesus, kid, that's everyone's family. The whole damn world is falling apart. That's why I carry this…"

The cabbie flashed a pistol over his right shoulder that looked nearly as old as him. It was either a prop for someone scared shitless or justice on the road. We skidded to avoid a mattress left by some asshat on the side of the road and the cab fishtailed. The pistol dropped on the passenger seat as he used both hands. My stomach lurched and I grabbed the headrest in front of me. I didn't normally use seatbelts in civilian life, but I buckled myself in like we were in an AH-64 Apache catching enemy fire. Hold your shit together, Jesus. Perdido Pines was close. I could almost smell the musk of the trailer park from here.

An SUV was parked on the shoulder of the road ahead of us, the passenger door open. From inside the vehicle, a plastic bag flew out and landed in the brush. Dark spots danced in front of my eyes.

"Pull over," I said. "I need to take care of something."

"Jesus, don't throw up," the cabbie said.

Brakes squeaked. The radio cut between stations. The cabbie veered over onto the shoulder behind the SUV. I flung open the door and approached the driver-side door.

"Why the hell are you littering?" I said to a man whose hair was tied in a topknot and whose beard dangled like an appendage.

"Jesus? What the fuck?" the man said, twisting to face me.

"You didn't answer my question." I caught my reflection in the passenger-side mirror. I couldn't stand looking at myself. Never could. I head-butted the side mirror three times in succession and heard a crack on the third try. I hoped it was the plastic unit now dangling from wires above the wheel well and not my skull. "You should be more careful, asshole."

"I was trying to find my kid's inhaler, okay? Jesus, I'm sorry."

In the back seat, I thought I saw a pair of tiny legs gyrating through the tinted glass. What the fuck? I backed away. I felt the wetness on my cheeks and, at first, I thought it was blood, but it wasn't. I was tired and not in control of my emotions. A duffle bag landed at my feet from the window of the cab passing by. The man in it tipped an imaginary cap and burned rubber. Abandoned. Better, I suppose, than being shot.

"Hey, man, do you know where Perdido Pines is?"

Shocked, the man pointed diagonally across the field where an access road had a faded sign advertising mobile homes available to lease or buy. I flung the duffle bag over my shoulder. An engine roared behind me. Tires squealed on asphalt and thumped until the sounds receded. My head hurt and the wind tickled my two-day growth of beard. Finally, I was alone except for the tiny shadow that followed me in the reeds at the edge of the field.

To get to the access road I had to backtrack to where the mattress had been dumped. It looked almost new, perhaps the recent casualty of flying out of the back of a moving truck. It took everything I had to not simply lie down and sleep away the rest of my days. Maybe I would wake several years from now with a beard as long as the man I'd scared, the military no longer looking for me, no one looking for me.

It reminded me of the time Solomon and I decided to help Dirty Harry. He was a homeless man we passed to and from middle school on the days we decided to attend. Solomon was my best friend back then. Our parents stuck together and set up shop with the rest of the *Aces* crew in a revolving set of apartment complexes in and around Lake Charles. It was far enough away so that the dirty dealings on the river could be kept separated from spouses and kids. At least that was the theory. Me and Solomon excelled at getting in trouble, getting high, and getting in over our heads. We sometimes shot the shit with Dirty Harry, who was an ex-sailor who'd traveled the world, at least we thought so by his tattoos with the faded letters of languages I didn't know. He played harmonica and set out a shoe box he told us was for food money, but we knew it mostly went to booze.

One night we rode our bikes through an alley behind a mattress store and saw a mattress had been tossed in the dumpster. We asked the owner of the store if we could take it for a friend and he laughed. That's when we decided to come back at first light and show him the true meaning of charity. Solomon told me he was just protecting our source for beer. Dirty Harry did make runs to the liquor store for us but underneath I knew he was proud about doing something for someone else. It didn't come as easily to him as it did to me. We had too many teachers in black market living to understand that there are some lines you don't cross. In fact, we barely ever saw them. Our childhood was all murk and untrustworthy memories.

We'd left our bikes at home and picked up a couple of shopping carts at Kroger along with a pair of bolt cutters in my gym bag. It took us nearly ten minutes to clip the lock on the back gate and to balance the twin mattress sideways across two carts. Progress away from the store was slow and we could hear a man swearing behind us as we turned the corner. Luckily the storeowner was overweight and out of shape. He chased us for two blocks. Even with the need to balance our load he never caught us. It took Dirty Harry a while to get used to the softness of the mattress.

Afternoon was ending and I felt my strength returning to me. I unwrapped a black bandanna from my knuckles and wiped my forehead. The cloth was damp, but I couldn't tell what was sweat and what was blood. The gravel access road ended, and I started looking for the address I'd memorized. My family curse felt strong in the twilight, and I knew I wasn't alone in this trailer park. Every curse was the curse of America, of men who

fled, fought to be free, battled their own natures, and everything in between. The sounds of night were already starting,
the crickets and bullfrogs, and dogs braying at wild creatures
rustling in the woods. In the low bodies of the trailers, lights
flickered and families argued, either on TV or in real life. Did
it really matter which was which? Soon I'd have to explain to
Deirdre that I was heading out West to help Solomon and that
she was engaged to a guy trying to hide from himself and the
US government.

No sense putting off the reunion any longer. I trudged
toward the home I had bought with wages from my time overseas. Half-dead planters of herbs hinted at Deirdre's haphazard
cooking and inability to keep anything alive. White paint curled
up on the porch and mailbox, and one of the trashcans had
been knocked on its side. Part of me wished that I had stopped
to peek through the trailer curtains, or to knock on the door. I
was too tired and too eager to confess my sins to Deirdre, only
to discover, with a turn of the nob, that she had worse ones to
confess to me.

3

SHADOW IN THE REAR VIEW

"Buddy" is a kid's name, a dog's name, not a name for a man. Deirdre didn't actually say these words, but the message was clear when she didn't bother to cover herself up. I stood there, idiot that I was, in the doorway of the trailer, transfixed by her straight black hair spilling down her arched back. She didn't have on a stitch of clothing. Normally, not a bad homecoming, right? Problem was that she wasn't alone inside the trailer. My uncle Mad Miles Rivet, at least, looked pleased to see me. He waved awkwardly on one side of Deirdre's hips straddling him on the black leather couch and poked his head around the other side.

"Goddammit, you were supposed to spend the night in Fort Polk," Miles complained.

Jesus, as though that explained why he was banging my girl-friend and betraying someone who was his flesh and blood. I looked away from the couch to take in the trailer decor. It was a thrift-store museum of mismatched boat relics, walls lined with buoys, fish mounted on the walls with mouths agape, posters of ocean tragedies from the *Titanic* to the *Edmund Fitzgerald*. The carpet was the color of a polluted green sea, and the walls were the shade of an overcast sky with a stucco white ceiling serving as a single cloud mass above us. Deirdre thrived on the depth and depression of the sea. To her, mermaids were the ghosts of those who'd drowned. This is what she'd assumed happened to my parents and part of why she'd been drawn to me in the first place.

Miles started to shift out from under Deirdre, but she shook her head at him before staring over her shoulder at me. "There's no need to hide what's going on anymore."

"Anymore?" I asked, the door wide open behind me. It was as though the entire world could see my embarrassment.

"Do I really need to spell it out?" she asked.

"I got conned. Fair enough. I always knew who you were. I just thought I was in the inner circle."

I thought back to the months I spent shacking up with Deirdre in my senior year of high school and how her absentee parents had given us our first taste of playing house. My folks had gone missing in a hurricane that ravaged the poorly named town of Lucky, Mississippi. The Category 4 storm had destroyed the moored riverboat, *Aces*. We'd been going out casually until my parents' disappearance. It wasn't long after that when the landlord served notice on the apartment I'd shared with my folks. Moms and Pops had already been behind on rent and I had no choice but to vacate. I had few options available with my uncle Miles still finishing a stint in a Shreveport jail. Deirdre had given me a place to stay while I slept-walked my way through my senior year of high school. She became what I thought was family.

Now my new and old family both looked like they were doing just fine without me.

"You left me," Deirdre said. "What did you think was going to happen?"

"I don't know," I said. "I figured we'd sort it out together."

"I've already sorted it out. You found spending your life with me scarier than going halfway around the world to a warzone," Deirdre said.

She was right, of course. How could I blame her when I'd already checked out of our relationship? My plan to move on to California without her had happened even before I went AWOL.

"Hey, aren't you being tough on the kid?" Miles asked Dierdre.

My uncle was a completely different matter. I balled my fist and felt the urge to pummel him. Miles had always been in Pops' shadow, looking for opportunities to one-up him in the ways of brothers. Maybe this is why I absorbed my twin. Miles was a weak man easily swayed by others. I was paralyzed in a way I'd never been in Afghanistan by whistling mortars or RPGs.

"This is all my fault," I said.

"C'mon, Buddy, you can do better than that if you want to win her back," Miles said.

"Shut up," Deirdre and I said simultaneously.

We smiled at each other, by impulse, by the rhythm you get living with a woman and sharing tastes in books, music, TV. Then the moment was memory again, a reminder of what we'd once shared.

"I needed some time to get my act together," I confessed. "I still need some time, I suppose."

"Take all the time you need," Deirdre said. "Just not in my place."

There it was out in the open. *Her* place. I'd sent her my paychecks during my tours in Afghanistan, which she'd used as a down payment on the damn trailer. At least my uncle had been able to enjoy the digs, probably in between his favorite pastime of running booze on weekends into a handful of dry counties in the middle of the state.

"I won't be back," I said.

"Why don't you take your loser uncle with you? He's just about served his purpose."

Miles grumbled and lifted his massive frame, turning sideways so that he could slide out from under Deirdre. He mooned me before sprawling on the floor next to the couch. "Dammit, girl, I'm not a piece of meat."

Deirdre laughed. "Wasn't that what I was?"

Watching my inebriated uncle fumble for his clothes floating on the sea-green carpet among beer bottles and last night's takeout, I almost felt sorry for him. The rogue found his wrinkled Hawaiian shirt. His jeans were by the door, at my feet. I shifted my duffle bag over my shoulder, reached down, and picked up the worn black denim. Bingo. I transferred his keys to my own cargo pocket and flung the pants over Miles's head.

The belt buckle clanked against the large-screen TV. I'd always hated how Deirdre needed to have the TV on while we slept. Hell, I was surprised that she hadn't been watching the tube while having sex with my uncle.

"What's so goddamn funny?" Deirdre asked.

"The little things," I said.

She gave me a pained look. Maybe her revenge was just a cover to make me miserable and needy, to put me back in her depressive care. I waved goodbye and blew her a kiss in lieu of a great last line. Her thin fingers, with chipped black nails, shook in a fist before she presented me with the bird. Primal. No last words. Perfect.

By then, Miles had managed to get one leg into his jeans. He was hopping around like a kid learning the rules of hopscotch. Deirdre's expression turned to embarrassment. Was it for herself, my uncle, or both? She covered her chest with her arms, aware now of the open door.

I turned to face Miles. "Sorry for taking your truck. Should just about settle our score."

"That's cold, kid. The Pope himself would have tapped that," he said, jerking his thumb behind him and dodging a return kick from the couch. He accidentally stuffed his left foot in the same pant leg as his right and stumbled. I turned and ignored the thump behind me. The sound was followed by a string of swear words, first a male voice, then female, then intermixed. I walked out beneath a murky sky to the red Ford pickup that had known more than its share of law-breaking and accidents. Grand theft auto wouldn't phase the vehicle one bit. I jumped in the truck, gunned the engine, and aimed the car hard to the right. I bounced in the seat as I destroyed a flower box and sped across the neighbor's lawn. I didn't look back at my home-that-never-was in Perdido Park and tried not to think what might have been. It was time to leave my childhood behind. There was wreckage behind me that stretched far beyond torn-up flowers and pieces of wood. There were pieces of myself only visible in the rearview. I felt the danger of looking back and crashing in the here and now.

It was nearing three a.m. when the gas warning light started blinking on the truck dashboard. Maybe I shouldn't have tried to put Texas in the rearview in a single sitting. I charted my course across the state by smell. The muskiness of the gulf coast and fumes from factory towns shifted to the stench of cattle housed for slaughter. Finally, the flat terrain began to curl where Highway 10 dipped just a few miles from the Mexican border. The truck was running on fumes, and I didn't have a clue how long it would take me to find a twenty-four-hour gas station. I exited the empty highway onto an off-ramp marked Avocado Street. It looked like I was on the outskirts of a border town. I pulled off the road into the first lot I could find and veered into an alley between a closed roadhouse diner and an out-of-business video store. I stared at the indecipherable graffiti on the windows of *Video Varmints* as though it was a message from a deity or a time-traveling version of myself.

I laughed at my own stupidity just before collapsing into sleep, the kind where you wake every few minutes but are still able to dream. I found myself back where I'd started my journey in the prisoner compound in Kabul, finishing up my final night shift guarding POWs. The Bagram Internment Facility, a converted former Soviet airfield, was quieter than usual. Only a handful of guards watched over the hundreds of prisoners sleeping a dozen to a cell. We would be moving them soon to another building into the care of Afghans, and the prisoners were anxious. I sat naked in a folding chair outside the shared cells, taking a sponge bath. The showers were too damned far away, I guess. Not sure why I was naked. The Bobs, our names for the prisoners dressed in matching blue jumpsuits, were awake as though disaster was imminent. They watched me run the sponge over my limbs and torso. They watched me like I was a savior. They watched me until I rubbed my skin raw.

"You better hurry," Niles said in the cell next to me. He had a British accent from his days in London before his father dragged them to Pakistan to help his uncle in the export business. Niles was about my age and was known by everyone, military and prisoners alike, for his skills in English, knowledge of American culture, and his six-month tenure at the airbase. Niles had made himself indispensable to try to keep himself from following his uncle and father to GTMO.

"Why should I hurry?"

"Because you don't want to see this," Niles said. "It's moving day. And there's going to be a few scores settled."

"Sure you're not paranoid?" I asked.

"I'm pretty sure a man in jail has reasons to be paranoid."

The interrogators had warned us not to engage with the prisoners, but the hours on duty were monotonous and Niles was talkative. He shared tales of growing up in London after moving there from Egypt. If he was a liar, I never was able to catch him at it. He was studying to become a doctor when his father pulled away his funding unless he joined him. The trip lagged on for several weeks, and they moved locations several times. Sometimes, without warning, he was asked to dress the wounds of some of his father's friends. He hadn't asked how pieces of metal had made their way into their bodies. He could do very little except to make sure the men didn't get infections or bleed out. Yes, he admitted, he should have refused, but was worried he'd be left without funds to return to London. This was his fault, his complicity in helping terrorists.

Niles has spent months sharing details of everywhere he'd been and identifying photographs. He had helped the interrogators map the stories of other prisoners, and his intelligence was trustworthy enough that he had been given a single cell. This was partially to protect him from the other POWs, an amenity that would soon be ending. While the interrogators treated him like a younger brother, the MPs, especially Staff Sergeant Lasicky, hated his guts.

I wasn't very popular among the other guards, either. They

thought I was weird for taking the night watch and for the countless books I devoured in poor lighting. Niles and I ended up spending way too much time together. We'd even shared plans to catch up after he was freed to return to his mother in London, and I was no longer in the service.

Lasicky appeared in the hallway and relieved me for the last time, his flashlight clacking along the cell doors, stirring the other prisoners awake. He loved getting under my skin. Once he realized that messing with the prisoners bugged me, it became his favorite pastime. Lasicky was the classic bully, and he had an endless supply of victims. Tonight, he had a devilish look in his eyes. Still, I walked past him with eyes averted and left the cells for the last time.

"Good luck with Deirdre. I'll see you in London," Niles called out.

"You'll see him in hell!" Lasicky yelled, kicking over the chair I'd been sitting in. Inexplicably, he stripped as I had, and the prisoners did not avert their eyes or turn away. The only thing left was his flashlight and keys dangling from his fist.

"Hang in there, Niles!" I called out, but my voice came out as a whisper. Sound did not penetrate the shadows at the main doors, opened for my departure. What was I supposed to do? I trudged outside and took in the mountain range, lit up with the new sun. The ridges displayed shades of red in between the vertical lines in the rock, like blood soaked into the land from its history of conflict. I headed to my quarters, suddenly without purpose. It would take me less than an hour to place every possession I owned into a single bag and board the plane home. I left my books in the common area for the soldiers still left behind. Who was I now that I wasn't looking out for the safety of prisoners?

I blinked my eyes and the sun was now invading the windshield of the truck. A lawnmower, from some unseen location, throttled its engine and I tried to place where I was in the world. My throat was as parched as the gas tank of the truck. Outside, a plastic bag roamed the asphalt mesa, traveling west like me on its migration toward a homeland in the Sargasso Sea.

I was stiff and nearly stumbled stepping out of the truck. My back ached and my ass was sore from the hours of sitting on a plane, in a cab, and now in a stolen truck. One thing was clear—if I wanted to make it to LA to see Solomon, I was going to need to get my hands on some cash. I didn't own a credit card. Even if I did, I wasn't about to use it or a debit card at an ATM. No way was I going to provide anyone with a trail to track me. I leaned back into the car to see if Miles had stashed any cash in the glove box. What I found was something that was almost as good in these parts.

4

Shadow Aim

I waited in line inside the *Super Budget Gas Station & Food Mart* behind a middle-aged woman in a tight pink tracksuit. The fluorescent lighting was brighter than the sun peeking out over the parking lot. She cleared her throat before plunking down her items on the counter next to a buckling cardboard display for herbal stimulants. I had bad BO and even worse breath. I unwrapped my last piece of gum and tossed it almost to the ceiling before catching it in my mouth.

Pops always had an unerring aim. It went beyond his skill with bar games like darts and pool. Or the ability to toss a crushed beer can in the trash can from any room or any angle. He also had the ability to target people who wanted to hand him their money and women willing to give him just about everything. He was disappointed that I did not have this kinetic talent. The closest I came to it, I suppose, was my fists.

On my sixteenth birthday, my father surprised me with a fake driver's license. Little did he tell me that he would soon have me hauling booze for Uncle Miles, one of their many side scams. We had my first official drink in a bar, something I didn't have a chance to do when I turned twenty-one during my latest tour. He was the one who got drunk. He'd won a hundred-dollar bet, with hundred-to-one odds, making a bull's-eye with a dart from his seat at the bar. He ordered me to drive him home. We took back roads to avoid the cops and he told me different versions of stories I'd heard before.

I hadn't yet learned to drive all that well and was focusing on keeping the car in my lane. Not sure whether I was distracted by my father's chatter or my worry about the approaching headlights, but I saw the stop sign late and skidded to a stop. The nose of our car was partway in the intersection, but no harm was done, no cross traffic.

"Christ, son, you made me spill my beer," Pops told me, and pawed at the Bud splashed on his lap. I looked at him for a moment. Over his shoulder I saw a shirtless man emerge from the woods and charge the car.

"Help," the man cried out, his eyes crazy and wide. He launched himself on the hood of the car and clung to it like driftwood in a river we could not see.

"It's a scam. His friends are going to jump us," Pops said. "Get out of here, dammit!"

I could hear the screams of several men from the woods, and I punched the accelerator. The man slid along the hood, and I heard the crack of the passenger's side mirror smack him in the ribs and fling him in a ditch. I wanted to go back around to check on whether the guy was okay but Pops just sipped his beer and turned on the radio. "We Rivets don't get conned," he explained, and I couldn't help but think about how badly I'd hurt the man or if he'd really been trying to flag us down for help.

"Hey, buddy, you're next."

My name jolted me, even out of context. A goateed clerk, with a tattoo of a red spider on his forearm, put down his book *The Green Ripper* by John D. McDonald. I stepped to the counter and he rang up a Styrofoam cup of coffee with the consistency of spent motor oil. I left exact change but that wasn't the reason for my visit. I opened my mouth but the bell on the door stopped me.

Heavy footsteps approached the cash register and a gravelly voice belted out behind me. "Chief's working today and you know what that means?"

I turned to see who was giving the cashier shit and it was a guy my own age, with long greasy brown hair, pale skin, and a checkerboard flannel shirt unbuttoned to his navel over black-board shorts with skulls on the pockets.

"Free shit for us!" his friend joined in, or maybe it was his brother, as the dude had the same thin face and oily pelt, covered by a camouflage T-shirt, hunting cap, and faded blue jeans. This was one of those gas stations off the highway that made customers prepay for gas. It was a gesture of mistrust in the nature of people and these fucktards made me understand why.

"You should probably get out of here," the kid behind the counter said, and noticed his skin was several shades darker than mine. "I can handle these assholes."

"You shouldn't have to," I said, walking over to the dumbatic duo pawing at beer in the cooler. "First punch is on me, but after that you guys have to pay."

Both guys sized me up and I knew I had a few moments to make an impression. I balled my right fist and popped myself hard in the mouth, enough to feel the sting and for blood to well up.

"Psycho," one of them said, and I knew the fight was over. I smiled at the hicks and imagined blood on my teeth. "You call that a punch?" I asked, laughing loudly.

"You're a demented Harry Potter," the other one said, and they bolted, leaving their haul on the counter and racing to their car. I thought I saw a shadow scurry in the corner behind the chips and corn nuts. A cat of some kind, perhaps? More likely, I was starting to lose it.

"What did that asshole mean by that Harry Potter comment?" I rummaged through a sunglasses display to replace the ones that had been crushed yesterday, and found a pair of aviators that fit perfectly on the bridge of my nose.

"You have a red scar on your forehead like a lightning bolt," the clerk said. "It's obvious you scared the shit out of them."

I'd held napkins from the hot dog dispenser to my lips and pinched down to stop the flow. "Most people don't like the sight of blood."

"They're just a couple of bullies. Went to my high school and are still losers."

"Didn't those guys saying 'chief' bother you?"

"They want me to get mad," he said. "It pisses them off when I ignore them."

"I've never had patience for bullies," I said.

"I'm pretty sure they saved themselves from a world of pain. You look like a fighter."

"I'm not THAT good," I said. "I've practiced a few martial arts, but I've never found one I loved."

"Story of my life. Just switch out martial arts for women," the clerk said.

"My last year in Afghanistan, I ended up studying krav maga with one of the Special Forces guys. It combines judo, boxing, jujitsu, aikido."

"Name's Owen," he said.

"I'm West." There it was. My new name. The direction I was headed.

He looked at the glasses on my forehead. "So, what can I help you with?"

I hadn't yet worked up the courage to ask him for a favor on the wrong side of legal. "Do you like that book? Isn't that from the author who wrote Cape Fear?" I gestured to the paperback on the counter with a finger pointing like a gun.

"I'm addicted. This is my third time reading *The Green Ripper*. It's about a detective, Travis McGee. He has a knack for saving the day and never getting paid."

I understood addiction. I was a serial reader. Once I liked a book from a given author, I was rabid. I read each book one after the other before I moved to the next. Currently, I was absent both a girlfriend and an author. I'd finished reading *Goodbye Columbus* in a reverse trajectory of the writer's career in my overseas Philip Roth addiction. "I'll have to check it out someday."

"Here," Owen said, tossing me the book. "You here for gas? I don't see a truck outside."

"It's parked around the corner," I admitted. "I'm out of gas and I have a proposition. Can you close down shop for a few minutes?"

"Is what you're asking legal?" Owen asked.

"Nope."

"Okay, now I'm interested."

Owen gestured for me to head out the front door. The bell rang behind me and my eyes watered from the dust whipping across the asphalt. There were no people anywhere in sight—at the station, on the road, on the freeway overpass. Owen paused to lock up the convenience shack. He followed me across the adjoining lot to the alley where I'd parked the truck. The mid-morning sun was now beaming across the dented bed, and I could see more clearly that the truck, like me, had seen better days. Wordlessly, Owen trailed me to the passenger door. I unlocked the truck and opened the glove box, revealing three pistols of varying models and ages. I wasn't a gun expert, far from it. The only weapons I'd ever shot were in the military. I had no idea of their worth and was at the mercy of whoever bought them from me.

"These stolen?" Owen asked.

"I can guarantee it. My uncle always shaves off the serial numbers. No one will be looking for these, but these aren't the types of guns you can register."

"What do you want for 'em?" Owen asked.

"Whatever you'll give me. I need enough gas to get to LA to help out a friend. If you throw in a pair of sunglasses, I'd appreciate it."

"I know a few people looking for some peace of mind with a piece of this kind."

"That's damn poetry," I said.

"For Texas it sure as hell is." Owen stuck out his hand and we shook, the ritual of agreement still a necessity. The gripping of hands was a leftover from days when it seemed a good idea to see if the other guy was carrying a weapon. Owen told me to hang tight while he secured the funds. It gave me a chance to take a piss between the truck and the wall. The yellow stream sent a lizard scurrying out from the shadows. Twin ridges exposed darting eyes as he stuck his head out into the sun, exposed like I was. He didn't wait to discover the source of the precipitation and took off, looking for new shelter. Humans were animals, and animals all had instincts, whether we followed them or not. I needed to follow the critter's lead and disappear underground somewhere in LA until I could figure out my next move.

5

BORDER SHADOWS

With two hundred bucks in my cargo pants, several bottles of water tossed into the glove box to replace Uncle Miles's illegal firearms, and a pair of cheap aviator sunglasses, I embarked on my journey. I migrated westward alongside tourists, Native American ghosts, the spirits of gold panners, and hucksters fueling me with the zeal of manifest destiny and a twinge of something that might be the onset of depression. Outside, the long day burned as though a distant fire were burning up the bowl of America. Unlike other travelers, I wasn't trying to discover something, pursue a long-distance romance, or become rich. My dream was to keep my only friend in the world safe and to escape attention in the pileup of cars near the ocean, to disappear beneath waves of people crashing over one another into the murky ecosystem on the dark floor of the city, out of sight.

I thought about my long-ago brother, the twin I'd absorbed in the womb. Was lil' bro protecting me somehow from the firstborn curse of my family? My father Louis had thought so. He was also convinced that he had figured out the mathematics of Keno, much to the detriment of the family finances. My mother Louise thought that it was hilarious how he took money from suckers all day yet was one himself. Moms was a firecracker in her own right. Her love of combining booze and pills was a special kind of Molotov cocktail that consumed those around her at odd moments of the day or night. In many ways, I'd always felt like the adult in the family. Not uncommon among my friends growing up, Pops and Moms had been ill-prepared for my entry into their lives.

Louis and Louise, kindred spirits brought together by their

names and love of chaos, were no Thelma and Louise. They were survivors, through and through. They conned everyone around them—acquaintances, friends, and family—to fuel their vices. They were so much fun to be around that often folks didn't complain when their wallets got a little lighter in the process. I had a hard time imagining them not finding a way to survive under any circumstances, even a random act of nature. The family curse, after all, was one of long-suffering. After the hurricane, when their bodies hadn't been found, I gradually began to accept their departure from my life. I mourned my folks just as I had the brother inside of me, but I felt adrift. My exodus was tenuous at best with the army and Deirdre now firmly planted in the rearview mirror.

Outside, the daylight scared the crap out of me. Even though I doubted Uncle Miles had reported his truck stolen, I felt exposed in the way of ancient desert travelers. We were on the brink of summer solstice. I felt the need to haul ass across the western states to avoid getting crisped. For a day and a night, I did nothing but pump my car and my body with cheap fuel and speed through the remainder of Texas, New Mexico, and Arizona. I crossed over into California before dawn and almost decided to pull over. The lack of funds meant that a motel was out of the question, and I didn't want to spend another second in the truck—waking or sleeping—than absolutely necessary.

I thought about all my favorite travel novels and my journey took on a dreamlike quality. Would I discover strange new people on my journey, where I would be either a lumbering giant or a midget tossed around like a doll? Would I be shipwrecked with no escape, no one to talk to, and no place to flee the elements and my own dubious nature? Would I come into the town on a hero's quest to correct some injustice? Or would I simply disappear into obscurity like an old book that had fallen out of favor?

It's funny what crosses your mind in the borders between states, between wakefulness and sleep, between being a boy and a man. Why didn't I feel more solid? Everyone around me grabbed life with gusto while I felt like an observer, a journalist, unsure of setting foot on the scales of life. Books had always been my vice even in school where letter grades hadn't mattered to me. Even the jobs I'd had, such as they were, from babysitting the kids of the *Aces* crew to signing up in the army as an MP, were passive activities, watching over others.

I'd learned early on to hide my money and belongings from my folks. When Pops used the cash from hawking my baseball card and comic book collections as gambling seed money I gave up on both pursuits. Moms siphoned my babysitting stash to buy booze, and I started to get savvy about hiding my loot. My favorite spot to hide away cash was in the pages of *Mark Twain*. It was of the few possessions I kept over the years.

Perhaps Buddy actually *was* a dog's name. I had watched over my parents but not nearly well enough. I then traveled halfway around the world to watch over prisoners as helpless as the marks getting fleeced on the gambling riverboat. There was never black or white in either place, just many non-sexy shades of gray.

If a caterpillar turns into a butterfly and a boy into a man, what exactly did a bulldog like me transform into? How many others wandered the earth feeling more animal than human? Perhaps now that I was leaving Buddy behind, West could make better sense of the world as it was. West was a man on the run. West was a madman operating without sleep. West was someone who spoke about himself in the third person and could be the man I'd always feared I'd be.

Not long after sunrise, traffic slowed at a checkpoint. I wanted to park the car on the shoulder of the highway and escape into the desert, but West wouldn't let me. I drove up to a booth in the far-right lane beneath a yellow sign with black letters that read *California Inspection*. What in God's name did that even mean? I pulled up and stopped at a kiosk to my left and rolled down my window. The guy in the booth wore a short-sleeve blue shirt, but it didn't appear to be a uniform. He had odd patches of hair on his unusually long face, either growing in a bad beard or losing some kind of work dare. What kind of inspection was this? He better not ask to see my license or registration.

"Where are you coming from?" he asked.

"Kabul," I replied.

"This isn't a joke, kid."

"Sure isn't. I just got home from Afghanistan. I'm on leave to go visit my family in LA." This was only a half lie as Solomon was as close to family as anyone I had.

"Are you carrying any fruits or vegetables into the state of California?" he asked, and I looked at him oddly. It blew my mind that he was worried about bugs sneaking into the state without worrying about dangerous human parasites looking to take root here. Both of us had our windows open. The space between us shimmered as though even the air had collided with insects and carried smudges of death. Maybe I was just seeing spots from the energy shots and lack of sleep. "Do you have anything living in the car that you are bringing across the border?" he asked, more loudly this time.

Good question. Was I really alive? Hard to know. Finally, I shook my head vigorously with a "no sir" and pointed my forefinger at the inspector. The dude ran his non-clipboard hand through his thinning hair and squinted his eyes at what I assumed was the lightning scar on my forehead.

"You ever read Harry Potter?" he asked.

"No, sir. The books are labeled for young adults. I'm looking forward in life, not backward."

The man's face dropped in disappointment, as though he had something clever to say. "I don't read much but I sure enjoyed those. There's a kid who fights evil but he's part evil."

"Sounds like the story I'm in. Only the villain is me," I said, feeling the fog of not sleeping surrounding me. Maybe that's all magic was. Breaking through the border between sleep and dreams, life and death.

"Take care of yourself, kid. And get some shuteye. Your family is waiting for you."

"On the other side," I said, thinking about how my folks had passed on but then realized he was talking about California. I chuckled and put the car into gear.

"Thank you for your service," he said, waving me ahead. Maybe I'd misjudged the guy. It had to suck pulling people over and rifling through their shit. I accelerated slowly until the inspection station was out of my line of sight. A few minutes later, I wondered if it had been a mirage, some passage on a hero's quest, or a power play from a federal agency desperate to keep its funding. Most likely, it was all those things. I decided to leave all caution to the wind and haul ass to LA.

In Solomon's last letter, he talked about his gig as a DJ. The bar was called Club Paradise, and it was on Olympic Boulevard. My love of Greek mythology had set the location firmly in my memory. I pulled off the freeway near the ocean and it only took me ten minutes of aimless driving until I turned on Olympic. Hot damn! Maybe my luck was turning. I immediately pulled over next to an intersection where a heavyset white guy in a wheelchair held court, shaking a cardboard sign that read, Injured Vet Needs Food.

LA already reminded me of New Orleans, where tourists and the homeless wandered the streets in each other's company. I rolled to a stop and parked the truck, ignoring a street sign with several warnings in green and others in red. The truck had paid its penance for my uncle Miles and had been a good travel companion. I would no longer need it. I waited for several SUVs to zoom by and climbed out. I stamped my boots to shake off the tingling in my legs from sitting for so long and reached back inside to get my few belongings from the passenger seat. Now what the hell was I supposed to do?

It was cooler outside than I expected in late June. Perhaps the ocean breeze was to blame for the chill that I felt from the damp T-shirt clinging to my skin. I rummaged inside my duffle bag and pulled on the first piece of clothing I could find. It was a black and silver *Saints* hooded sweatshirt from the *Aces'* lost-

and-found bin. I'd held on to it, not for my love of football, but for sentimental reasons. It was the only thing I still owned that Moms had given me.

I slung my possessions onto my back and adjusted the cheap sunglasses on my nose to protect myself from the mid-day sun. I slipped the paperback novel that Owen had given me into my cargo pocket next to my almost empty wallet and dog tags. I gripped the truck keys in my fist and wondered how long it would take for the truck to get towed. From here I could see where Olympic Boulevard dead-ended a few blocks from the ocean. It was clear that I needed to head east to find Club Paradise.

How far could it possibly be? Certainly not longer than the twenty-mile march, with full rucksacks, we'd been forced to do in basic training. Besides, I was stubborn. I flat-out refused to ask the tourists on the street corner to use their phones for directions. They stared at me alongside the man in the wheelchair and hurried across the intersection before the light turned. The vet lowered his sign and took me in. He rattled the coins in his KFC drink cup in a rhythm that must have matched his headphones blaring from a device in his jacket pocket. Were even the homeless in LA more wired than I was?

"Got any change to help an injured vet?" the guy asked, eyes glassy from booze, pills, or lack of sleep. His wheelchair looked almost new. His duds were military issue but from the wrong era, probably thrift store or army navy surplus.

"Where'd you get hit?" I asked.

"Stepped on an IED. Both legs got shredded."

"What unit?"

"The school of hard knocks," he answered, defensively, after an awkward pause. His eyes darted around him. I had seen every form of con in the company of my folks, in the *Aces* lounge, and on the streets of New Orleans with everyone from street performers to drunken college kids finding ways to steal you blind. Often, the body was used as bait. There's no way this guy served, and I wasn't about to let him off the hook.

"I've been there, man," I said, and dropped the truck keys into his cup and gestured to the vehicle I'd abandoned with a thumb over my shoulder. I figured he'd be stupid enough to get busted driving to his dealer's house or KFC in a stolen vehicle.

My new buddy sprang up from his wheelchair and lifted me off the ground with a bear hug. He held me there long enough for me to tell one group of tourists, "It's a miracle." The only real miracle is that I didn't throw up from the smell of whiskey and tobacco rising from his fatigues. Finally, he released me and broke into a happy dance with keys jingling. Finally, the "injured" vet plopped down in his prop, saluting me with the drunken swagger of a soldier on leave.

I turned my back and began marching eastward. Hopefully, Solomon had a place for me to crash. It felt damn good to be traveling with my own two legs instead of by plane or car. The heat was toothless and dry compared to Louisiana and I felt the freedom, the ghost weight of the flak jacket and Kevlar helmet I'd worn for so many months floating away like a bad memory.

6

Sunset Shadows

My mind wandered as I wandered eastward on Olympic Boulevard. I didn't know the address to Club Paradise and was confused by the signage in other languages. I passed an empty park with more dirt than grass and an office complex with a globe sculpture in a courtyard with a creepy post-apocalyptic vibe and a fountain that did not work. The buildings became shabbier as I trekked eastward. Industrial buildings cropped up alongside dingy mini malls filled with liquor stores, ethnic restaurants, and massage parlors. My new city was not kind to pedestrians. The sidewalks were cracked and strewn with garbage. Buses were few and far between. There also seemed to be many people sleeping on the sidewalk. Perhaps I should have been more concerned about getting an address and directions, and whether Solomon had actually managed to keep a job. I had reread his letter countless times, along with Deidre's, usually during my night shift rounds.

Our detention facility wasn't like the one to the south in Kandahar that operated 24-7. We interrogated our prisoners in the converted Russian airbase in daylight. I'd volunteered for the graveyard shift. I liked having the time alone to wander around the facility, sometimes on the ground level among the prisoners, other times on the walkway above. The other guards on duty hung out in the central station staring at cameras, chain-smoking and blasting music at full volume to soften up the harder prisoners for morning interrogators. At first, the other guards were friendly enough. Once I refused to play hearts, spades, poker, and other games of chance, I became an outsider. I became the weird guy who liked to pace. How could I tell them how I'd lost the urge to gamble before I'd even learned to shave? The army wasn't exactly a place to share childhood stories of hard knocks. That's why we all joined in the first place. Maybe I just didn't want to go through the headache of opening myself up. I avoided eye contact with the people I passed on the street and ate the last power bar from my cargo pocket. Time boiled in the air around me, in a desert that gave everyone the illusion of paradise. Just as I was thinking about trying to grab a few Z's on a bus bench, I found my destination. I'd just transitioned from a neighborhood of upscale businesses and apartment complexes to a stretch of warehouses beside railroad tracks when I saw the strange building that would come to haunt me. Welcome to Club Paradise—part castle, part strip club, with elements of fine stonework overlaid with cheap stucco and a mammoth neon sign facing the street.

This pale-blue building towered several stories above everything for blocks. It gave the distinct impression of a movie set in some alternate universe where a castle was the color of sky and sky was the color of stones. I would later find out that a Hollywood producer had erected this monstrosity as his homage to horror films before croaking mid-construction. Spooky details from the original concept remained: everything from stone ravens peering down from parapets, to twin towers on either end of the building, to a sunk-in brick driveway providing the illusion of a moat.

Beneath the blinking sign affixed on a fake castle drawbridge was a disheveled rock garden. It was strewn with cigarette butts and decorated with chipped alabaster statues of men and women in various states of disrobe and disrepair. You could see the holes where breasts, fingers, ears, and even balls once hung. Multiple owners had provided the building with a mishmash of influences, some layered into the architecture and others into the landscaping, all accented with graffiti that was partially and spottily painted over.

This place was whack. There was a cartoon image of a scantily clad woman atop the Club Paradise sign. She had a 1920s hairstyle and clothing, and kicked up one leg from a squat in a feat of gymnastic improbability. I was still surprised, though, when I went to the door and peered through the slit of black curtains. An erotic dancer dressed in white lingerie and a hoop skirt spun on a pole onstage. Her straight blond hair hung down in two ponytails to make her seem younger. She reminded me of some sad fairy-tale character. The ticket window was closed, probably too early for a cover charge…or a DJ for that matter. It might be hours before Solomon showed up, but at least I'd found the right place.

A shadow stirred from a wall alcove near the door just before I heard a gruff voice, "You lost or something? This isn't a hotel."

I took another instep inside the room and my eyes slowly adjusted. I faced a security guard in his midthirties with curly short-cropped black hair. He was a few inches taller than my six feet. Muscles spilled out of a short-sleeve black T-shirt that accentuated a bodybuilder's physique. I could sense him giving me the once-over, trying to determine whether I was a threat.

"I'm looking for Solomon," I said.

"Not here."

"We're buds and I just got into town. Can I hang here until he shows up?"

"I guess but sit your ass at the bar. Don't piss off the regulars or paw any of the girls until Solomon decides to show. He's probably still sleeping."

"He hasn't changed much then. I'm West."

"Deacon," the security guard said. "Welcome to LA. It's a town of opportunities. Even this shithole."

Walking into Club Paradise was like entering a different world. Deacon escorted me through an obstacle course of sin. Taking it all in was a little overwhelming, even with sunglasses on. Beside the main stage was a VIP room with long red velvet drapes pulled closed with a gold sash. The castle's interior decor provided an out-of-time feel even with the banks of dim track lighting illuminating the stages. Those tiny lights left the rest of the ground floor in shadow, except for the main oak bar beneath a gigantic chandelier. There were mythical creatures of all varieties etched into columns. I recognized a griffin, gargoyle, yeti, wolf, and sphinx. The mismatched creatures spanned different time periods and cultures.

The window overlooking the statue gardens framed two costumed women sipping drinks. One was a regal-looking woman in her midthirties, decked out in Egyptian garb, silver jewelry with oversized blue stones, and a straight black wig. She stroked the shoulder of a lithe, blond woman who appeared to be barely eighteen with a righteous combination of muscles and curves popping out of a skin-tight catsuit complete with ears and whiskers. They had sharp Eastern European features and luxuriated in the booth like a twin throne. Both stared at me imperiously, as though they ruled the castle and the souls of any men who wandered too close. Except for the contrasting hair colors, they could have passed for mother and daughter, an occurrence that undoubtedly had taken place once or twice in strip clubs around the country.

Club Paradise was the land that time forgot, a realm of lost props and movie star extras, and those drawn to the messy spectacle. There were doors everywhere and I would later discover that they led to the kitchen, the main office, the basement, the dressing rooms, the cooler, the west tower, and themed party rooms. There was rumored to be a secret passage that ran to the other half of the castle, where the owner and his family lived. There was an empty DJ booth with Mardi Gras beads hanging from the equipment and I could tell that Solomon spun there. At the bar was the kind of guy you'd expect to sling drinks in a place like this. He was in his late twenties, brown hair, perennial short beard stubble, good looks—a yet-to-be-discovered actor most likely, spending too much time chasing the wrong dreams and bagging the wrong women.

Deacon made a circuit around the main stage, watched guys flinging dollar bills at the bikini-clad woman in white, and then joined me. He pointed at the bartender. "That's Flynn." To Flynn, he said, "Hey, Flynn, got a newbie here for you. West is a friend of Solomon. Keep him out of trouble, will you?"

"Put your hands into your wallet for Alice, a Wonderland of a girl." Flynn belted out over the PA system. The bartender smiled at his own cleverness, returned a bottle of Maker's Mark to a shelf behind him, and spun to face me. He stretched out his right hand and practically vibrated with nervous energy. I dropped my duffle bag on the barstool next to me. He pumped my hand with energy and purpose. I returned the force with equal pressure for a few seconds. He released my hand first, though, and rubbed his knuckles. He looked me over and I found myself staring at his hairy chest and gold cross necklace dangling in the exposed cleavage of a black dress shirt unbuttoned to the navel. Was he religious or just making a fashion statement?

"You can tell a lot about a man by his handshake," Flynn said with a slight East Coast accent like he'd tried hard to bury it along with some past life.

"What is that exactly?" I asked.

"There are dozens of ways you can shake hands. Don't laugh. Scientists have studied the way people place their hands on top or on the bottom, grip hard or go limp, spread fingers or hold on too long. It can tell you everything about a person's character. I should know. I'm an actor/writer /bartender. It's triply my job to understand people."

And triply his job to be annoying, no doubt, but I found myself liking Flynn. "And what did you find out about me?"

"I don't know you well enough yet to share. My insights are powerful stuff. People can freak out on you, man. I used to do Tarot readings, but this is just as accurate."

"No doubt," I said, even though I had a few.

"What can I get you while you're waiting?" Flynn asked.

"Coke." I didn't much like drinking except when I wanted to get shit-faced drunk, and any booze now would send me tumbling to sleep. Flynn spun on his heels, clanked ice, nozzled brown liquid, and slid a tall glass over to me in a spastic display of bartending.

For the first time, I took in the group sitting at the bar, the regulars I'd get to know far too well in the days to come. Flynn, ever the MC, introduced everyone around me. "Here's the real Club Paradise, our cast of characters. Next to you is Irv, a retired Hollywood agent now an agent of anarchy. Beside him is Blake, former wiretapper now working in IT at his brother's printing company...long story. Next is Judd and he's almost as pretty as one of the Judd sisters, only he's an artist and he hates his dad."

"Fuck you, Flynn," Judd said without looking up from his notebook.

"You're not that pretty," Flynn fired back. "And last, but not least, our resident couple, Spokane and Salt, director and producer. They've shot a number of projects right here on location."

I looked down the line of stools and waved to a group that only had a casual interest in me, lost in conversation about some actress I didn't know. I'd never watched much TV and I always felt like I was at a disadvantage in conversations about pop culture. I took *The Green Ripper* out of my bag, sipped my Coke, and started reading, trying my best to avoid the eyes of the dancers and invitations for lap dances. The bar flies gossiped and the outer ring of booths slowly started to fill. I lost myself in a tale of a detective who infiltrated the world of a terrorist cult to extract the daughter of a client. He pretended to be dumb and slow, waiting patiently for an opportunity to turn the tables on the bad guys.

It was dusk when I decided to stop reading. I was halfway through the book; the writing was oddly addictive. I could already tell I'd read more in the series. I inserted a Paradise cocktail napkin into the spine of my paperback as a bookmark. Jesus, Solomon better show up soon. My eyes were fried from reading in the dim lighting in my attempt to avoid checking out the revolving door of exotic dancers on the main stage. I'd scarfed a rubbery chicken sandwich from the bar, and I was now officially out of money. I found myself eavesdropping on the conversation of the regulars. Apparently, they were producing a movie after hours at Club Paradise. From the sound of things, it didn't seem like this was the first time they'd worked together.

"I need more time with the script," Flynn said. "Genius takes time."

"It's a horror film, for fuck's sake. All you need's a good monster," old-time agent Irv muttered next to me, stroking his gray sideburns and stuffing a dollar bill from an endless roll into the costume of a passing Valkyrie bombshell. "And this bar's filled with 'em."

"We'll use newbies from our actors' workshop for bit roles," Salt said.

"Haven't they figured out yet that you're stealing them blind?" Blake took a break from pouring his shot of vodka slowly into a glass of 7-Up and covered his eyes with both hands for effect.

"Hasn't your brother figured out that you spend all day reading his emails and texts?" Salt asked, and she ran her fingers over Blake's fingers, but he yanked them away and curled them around his whiskey on the rocks.

"He doesn't even notice when I show up to work," Blake muttered.

"My dad doesn't even know I'm alive," Judd the artist added, scribbling furiously in his notebook. "Not that I care."

"That's why mama Salt is here," she said, blowing Judd a kiss. She turned and ran her fingers though Spokane's hair. The director flinched reflexively from the contact. Spokane was the quietest of the bar gang. He avoided talking in general and to Salt in particular. Spokane stared intermittently into his drink and into his phone, as though they were twin windows into some private hell. Perhaps all hell was private. I had a few questions about this group of people. Was Salt just Spokane's sugar mama who put together B movies to make him happy? Were any of them friends before bonding over bad drinks, bad dancing, and bad decor, or did the ambience of a stripper *Cheers* bring them all together?

"I've got a new design for the siren," Judd said. He held up his journal and displayed a combination drawing—part ghost, part vampire, all low cut and black.

"This is the first monster that I'm not playing," a voice behind me said, and it was Deacon, appearing out of nowhere. "Not sure why they're casting it as a female. Who's to say that a siren needs to be a woman instead of a sexy man like me?"

"I'm not sure I'm a good judge of such things," I said.

"You're the perfect judge. You're impartial at least, unlike this crew."

It was then I noticed the tall thin man, midtwenties, with a black hoodie standing on the far end of the horseshoe bar. The dude sipped a drink, eyes on the barflies and not on the dancers. He was the only other guy in the club with sunglasses on. I wasn't sure if he was a little buzzed, a little weird, or someone to keep my eye on. He blew me a kiss when he caught me staring at him, and I decided yes to all three.

There was something about this place that seemed all too familiar. This was a place where bottom feeders tried to survive on the dredges while even larger prey circled each other. There was also a United Nations of loneliness at work. The accents of the dancers in ridiculous costumes hinted at a melting pot of problems. My own guilt for abandoning Niles (and other prisoners) to abuse and endless imprisonment might not even be near the top of the list of sorrows at Club Paradise. You could sense a collective air of loneliness. Dancing women and bottomless drinks were not enough to wipe away collective despair. Somehow, this place felt way too much like home.

"Look who the cat, the dog, and the wolf dragged in," a familiar voice called out behind me. I knew it was Solomon, not just for the silky voice that he used to seduce women but also for his love of mangling common expressions. He looked the same as ever, except fitter, tanner, and blonder, with short-cropped hair bleached by the sun.

Before I could get off my barstool to give my best friend a hug, a shadow rippled beside me and gained momentum. Size: human form. I turned to see the hooded figure bull-rush my friend. He shouldered Solomon into Deacon, sending both tumbling into the DJ booth. Albums and CDs slid from aluminum shelves and onto Solomon's head. He was too stunned to lift his arms. Meanwhile, the hooded man placed his hands in his pockets and said, "DJ Dumbass, I warned you about what would happen if you stepped on my turf."

Deacon looked pissed, but he was having a helluva time untangling himself from beneath Solomon. Flynn reached behind the bar and lifted a worn wooden bat. I acted without thinking and yelled, "Hey, dipshit!"

The hooded man pivoted, and I could tell from the pissed-off look he was hopped up. Both hands shot out from the pocket of his hoodie and he lunged to place them around my neck. I stepped back and with one practiced martial arts move, I had his arms pinned against my chest. He shifted forward, just enough to keep him from toppling but not enough to aid him in getting leverage to muscle his way out of my hold. His face was inches from mine, and he snarled, "Let me go. No one fucks with Ricki Ticki and gets away with it."

"This creep isn't going anywhere," I said loudly, ignoring the threat. It was times like this when my dead twin seemingly gave me the strength of two men. "Deacon, get over here and check his pockets."

Deacon had already helped Solomon to his feet and he took his time searching the hooded attacker. He palmed the guy's sunglasses and crushed them into pieces with a single squeeze. Ricki Ticki's eyes were dark enough that I had a hard time seeing if his pupils were enlarged. He had a series of scars on his neck that looked like they could be from a wild animal. His features were a combo of white, Asian, and Latino, but his skin tone was closer to pink than brown or white. His round face and thin wiry frame seemed at odds, but there was no denying the dude was ripped beneath the sweatshirt. Damn, and he wore way too much cologne.

In the club, the music had stopped, perhaps from the damage to the DJ station. The bar flies were stuck to their stools, and probably pissed that they hadn't had the wits to video the scuffle. A heavyset man with a black beard the same color as his suit appeared at the top of the staircase and headed toward us with a sense of purpose. Solomon had finally gotten to his feet, and I could see that he recognized his attacker. Deacon lifted Ricki from his belt as easily as a kid, marched him outside, and tossed him out the front door. Solomon looked pale when the bearded man descended the staircase and ducked back inside his DJ booth to start straightening up.

On closer examination, the man was a giant, six feet five inches and well over three hundred pounds, with arms as big as my legs. His skin color was light brown, and he had vaguely Middle Eastern features. He was midforties, maybe older, but moved with the grace of a man who'd once been an athlete. The bearded man nodded at Flynn, who stashed away the bat and returned to serving customers. He followed me over to my stool and extended a paw that swallowed mine.

"Your friend Solomon can thank you for saving his job."

"How do you know—"

You don't need to know how I know things," the man interrupted. "I'm Zia Pourali, but everyone calls me Big Z. I'm the owner of Club Paradise."

"My name's West, and this place is anything but dull," I said.

Big Z's face crinkled in the corners of his eyes as he laughed. "That's exactly why I've come to talk to you. I have a proposition. I'm down one security man at the club, and I'd like for you to take the job."

"I have two conditions," I said.

"Shoot," Big Z said.

"I'd like to be paid under the table," I said.

"Not a problem."

"And I'll only work here if Solomon works here."

"Fair enough. I like your style. Direct. Like the way you dealt with that hood rat."

"Then do we have a deal?" I asked.

"Yes," Big Z said. "Get your ass here Monday at eight a.m. so we can give you a proper orientation."

I was glad that I didn't ask him what day that was. Big Z turned on his heels and marched into a back room behind the bar. All the patrons and club employees watched him, but it was the dancers who gave him their full attention, stopping mid-sentence and in one case mid-lap dance with a customer.

"He used to be a famous wrestler. He had his own commercials and was even in a few pictures," Deacon whispered, and I could see the allure that drew the muscular security guard to work here. He wanted to be a younger, more successful version of Big Z.

Metal coverings on the windows by the statue garden began whirring, followed by a set high above the front entrance. All the window shades began shutting electronically. Solomon wandered over once Big Z cleared the room and gave me a fist bump, but all I could think was how the club was closing its windows at sunset. It wasn't to block the low light pulsing in the western sky. It was to stop prying eyes in the darkness from seeing what was going on inside Paradise.

7

Hell Shadows

Even after spending most of the past few days without sleep, I woke before dawn on the stained futon couch of Solomon's one-bedroom apartment. His pad was the front, second-floor unit of a shabby 1960s stucco complex just down the road from Club Paradise. Solomon told me that he didn't like to drive in Los Angeles when he could avoid it. He'd rattled off reasons ranging from DUIs to crazy drivers to his ancient car before I drifted off minutes after landing at his pad. Sleep deprivation gives soldiers and moms more in common than you might think: a fuzzy alertness, paranoia that the world is plotting against you, and an understanding that calamity can strike at any moment. And we are both easily startled.

The neighbor's dog started barking and I almost dove off the couch. My first reaction had been to reach for a rifle and helmet I no longer had. Then it was clear: I was no longer perched in the Hindu Kush range surrounded by the extended fingers of the planet attempting to poke the sky. Instead, I was sinking into a hole of my own making in Los Angeles.

After my eyes adjusted to the light, my other senses began working in overdrive. I checked myself to see if I had been invaded by insects ranging from sand flies to otherworldly camel spiders. Nothing had stopped them from finding me in the dark in Afghanistan, not pesticides, concertina wire, machine-gun nests, mosquito netting. There were no new welts or ticks that needed to be crushed between my fingernails. I was safe, at least, from small creatures looking to do me harm.

One of my only friends in the army had been the base exterminator, Conrad. He worked the night shift like I did. He was a gangly Black kid from Atlanta with a Southern drawl, which he had not lost, unlike my own largely successful efforts to loosen all ties to the slang and twang of Lake Charles. Conrad had been responsible for reinforcing the perimeter, entryways, and quarters from small invaders. He'd spooled netting by the mile and poisoned all manner of creepy crawlies that slithered, hopped, and strafed soldiers in their sleep. Conrad sometimes joined me to read in the guard shack while the others played cards. He was set on becoming a scientist with the college money from his tour of duty. He mostly read nonfiction while I stuck to my obsession with novels. My own plans for college, like everything else, were a work in progress.

Outside, an occasional car rattled by. By then I'd grown immune to noise: the constant vibrations of soldiers' steps; flamboyant Pakistani jingle trucks from civilian contractors who used them to haul anything and everything; the snores of other men separated by folds of fabric instead of walls; the gurgles from the bowels of the Russian-built airfield that could have been Stalin's ghost; and helicopters, planes, and Humvees. Noises meant that you were not alone.

But there, in Solomon's apartment, I was stuck at sea level, stuck couch surfing, stuck without an identity because of my AWOL status. I could probably return to Fort Polk with a slap on the wrist, a demotion, and a few months in the poke. The longer I waited to face the music the lengthier my punishment would be. I'd love to say that I was acting like a child, but my folks had never actually given me any structure. The army had given me plenty, but it came with a cost that I no longer was willing to pay.

Solomon's computer monitor was the focal point of the apartment, filling in for a TV. Its speakers had blasted music until Solomon stumbled into his bedroom with one of the dancers from the club who'd tagged along. I got up and touched the mouse, and the computer blinked on with a background of psychedelic purple and red swirls. I clicked on a browser and decided to scan the latest headlines. This, at least, I could get used to—the internet connections in Kabul were slow, slower, and slowest depending on whether you wanted to talk to your family, get sports scores, or look at porn.

I occasionally surfed Craigslist in Lake Charles. This wasn't to check out the weirdness of my hometown or to connect with my friends. Posting messages there was our family's fail-safe whenever we got separated from each other. My old man had probably learned this trick from his stint in jail. We posted in the "Rants and Raves" section. The trick was to write a headline with the name of the person you wanted to reach—only backward. It had been more than three years since my folks had disappeared and I still checked online faithfully. I'd felt too stupid to post my own ad even while I kept an eye out for a headline containing *Yddub*. Today was different, though. I created an ad with my father's name *Siuol* as the headline. Beneath it, I posted: *What the hell?*

Maybe it was time to accept my folks were dead. I'd held out hope until now because they'd skated out of trouble before. Countless scams and quick reflexes had left them relatively unscathed. I didn't get off that easy, though. My uprooted childhood had left me no better prepared for life than a balloon at a child's party floating into the sky. The empty caskets placed in the ground after the hurricane had felt like a parlor trick, the age-old con of palming the ball beneath empty cups. Was it possible that while eyes were diverted at headstones, Louis and Louise had taken the opportunity to reboot and take their show back on the road? I imagined them in some cranny of America scamming the locals to get by, all while planning the perfect retirement score.

Feeling restless, I tiptoed into the bathroom and took a quick shower. I changed into jeans and a black T-shirt, and decided to make breakfast. I found one clean pan and prefab pancake mix. I estimated the directions on the back of the box in a coffee mug and I ended up using olive oil when there wasn't any butter. The smell of cooking made me realize just how hungry I was.

While I cooked, a male manikin in a hoodie watched me.

The department store prop stood at the head of a dining room table filled with dirty dishes, pot paraphernalia, and take-out boxes. Anyone looking to come in and rob the place would see the silhouette of a guy on guard duty. This I understood—Solomon and I had grown up in the same den of vipers.

A half-naked brunette with a single lock of blond hair slipped out of Solomon's bedroom and closed the door behind her. She didn't even feign modesty. She zipped up her leopard-skin outfit as though to make sure she didn't leave it behind not because she was worried about me staring at her boobs. The shock of blond hair stood out like it was on fire.

"Hey, can I have some of those?" she asked. "Smells good."

"Not sure if there's a clean plate."

"I've got this." She cleared a corner of the table. I stabbed the first two pancakes with a fork and dropped them on take-out napkins she'd spread out.

"Jesus, he's a slob," she said.

"Always has been. You Solomon's girlfriend?" I asked.

"No way. I'm a hit 'em and quit 'em kind of gal. He's got the best dope and he's cute enough I suppose."

"Name's West."

"Tarzana," she said, smacking her lips from the pancakes she was devouring. "I'm only shaking my ass at the club to get through college at UCLA. I'm finishing up a graduate degree in zoology. Although I think I'm learning plenty about animals with the fucked-up guys paying me for lap dances."

"How in the hell do you commit to a career?"

"Same way you commit to a man," she said. "It's next to impossible."

I began mixing a second batch and she wolfed down the pancakes in record time. She was efficient, snake-like in how she swallowed strips she ripped with her hands. I turned my attention to flip the pancakes still in the pan to keep them from burning.

"Be careful," she said between mouthfuls. "Solomon's got a way of dragging everyone into the fire with him."

"I'm used to the heat," I teased.

"Not like this."

I felt another figure in the room and stared at the blackness of the mannequin's eyes. It was mesmerizing. The dead space there was like the one on my palm. We all had this darkness in our pupils. We all had this hole that expanded over time and turned people stiff, into something less than human. I looked down at the table and Tarzana was gone. Weird. Had she said "goodbye" and I'd missed it? I smelled the smoke rising off the pan and headed to the stove. I turned off the burner and began eating one of the pancakes myself. The hole could sometimes be filled by food or drink or women. Mostly, you tried to forget it existed.

Solomon sat beside me as I drove his boat of a car, a gold 1975 Chevy Impala, to a DJ gig. The first half of the drive we didn't speak. I knew little about what was going on, just that it was mid-Saturday afternoon. Solomon pointed at the windshield and mumbled one-word directions, his index finger jabbing at the horizon. In between, he drummed on the dash with his index fingers in a rhythm that seemed familiar. A song I couldn't quite place. In this vast landscape, there was something frightening and small dogging us. I could feel the darkness bleeding from under the cars, the exhaust spooling in the air. The sky itself was a shadow. The sun could not poke through. It had no chance in Los Angeles, not really. Not even the closest star could find its way through.

"I'm done with the army. I'm through slowly killing myself," I said finally.

"So, you decided to kill yourself quickly?"

"Figured I'd learn from the master," I said.

"True dat," Solomon said. "I'm in rare form in LA. You'll see."

"Can't wait to get a few more scars looking after you." I rubbed the jagged red bolt just starting to heal on my forehead.

"You're a bull in China," Solomon said, mangling another

expression, leaving me to wonder if he was still high from the night before, if he was unraveling like I was.

I shared the details of the past few days. Punching out my sergeant. Going AWOL. Finding Deirdre and Uncle Miles in a scarier position than *The Human Centipede*. The guilt I felt from leaving those damn prisoners behind. I had no idea where I was going, except the houses began getting nicer, and I had a hard time navigating narrow passes as we climbed into the hills. Occasionally, I had to pull over to let other vehicles pass.

"What kind of place you spinning at tonight?"

"Private party. Expensive house. Lots of women."

"Does this have anything to do with this married chick you're seeing?"

"Yep. Her name is Mona and she's married to Big Z's brother Yar. She runs an institute called *Goddess Guides*. They have classes on enlightenment, and I don't understand a damn thing they say."

"What the hell are you mixed up with?"

"Weird-ass shit for sure. It's a cult of some kind just for rich women. She sets up workshops for them, sells them crap they don't need, and sets up spiritual gatherings where they seek enlightenment by taking drugs like ayahuasca."

"What the hell is that?"

"A hallucinogen. I took the real stuff once, but Mona doesn't mess with it anymore. Too complicated. She loads a cocktail of feel-good drugs in the tea she gives these ladies."

"Sounds like a rave," I said.

"It is…but for rich women. She gets five hundred bucks a head for these all-night spiritual workshops. The women get their buzz on and feel better about themselves."

"Sounds whack," I said. "Any time money and drugs change hands things can get out of hand."

"Nah. It's chill. Mostly. You'll see. I texted Mona and told her you'd be coming along for security. Sometimes one of the husbands or boyfriends tries to crash the party."

"Doesn't this compete with your gig at Club Paradise?"

"Nah, there's a second DJ working there tonight. You'll find that Big Z and his brother Yar share employees. It's all one big, twisted family enterprise."

He motioned for me to pull over outside the tall gates of a hillside house the color of olives or uniforms back when there was an enemy worth fighting. The spread was huge. Three stories framed the sky in an L shape with sweeping arches and wrought iron gates. The gates whirred open so that I had just enough space to pull inside. There were eyes on me for sure. Cameras. Who knew what else?

Solomon texted someone. "Open says me," he said with a grin on his face. "This is gonna get weird."

One day in LA and already I was in a slow-motion fall into nothingness. What in the hell was I getting myself into?

The mansion belonged to a woman who was not even at the event, away on some trip, but part of the Goddess Guides clique. Maybe the homeowner didn't even exist or existed in the way my alter ego, West, did. My mind was everywhere at once as I took in the opulence of a home with tall ceilings and gleaming hardwood floors, mammoth couches and throw pillows, and chairs that looked like they could hold the weight of the universe.

I helped Solomon set up his equipment by the pool. The head of Goddess Guides came by and handed us two drinks the color of honey. She introduced herself as Mona, a small bird-like woman, barely five feet tall with a saunter that pulled curves out of the ground and the sky. She had brown eyes and skin and was of Middle Eastern descent. She had a voice that squeaked like a mouse and she kissed me on the cheeks. Mona winked at Solomon and sashayed away, saying *hi* to the most recently arrived women. She wasn't human, more like a wave always looking to crest and Solomon was the person who'd be swallowed up when it did.

Solomon left me with a plate of appetizers and a playlist while he helped prepare tea in the kitchen. By then, nearly twenty women congregated in small groups, wandering in and out of the adjacent living room through open glass doors while a few lounged poolside. They wore loose clothing with expensive fabric in order to appear earthy and uncomplicated. Nearly an hour later, Mona and Solomon emerged with trays and set up a tea set with Native American designs on the outside table. Each guest sipped tea and I found myself wondering what the hell was in it. Solomon brought two cups back and I didn't argue. I clinked cups and gulped it down, tired and lost, unsure about anything.

The women got energized by the brew and Solomon disappeared in a sea of them. My own feelings of protecting him intensified. Many came by to talk to me about their relationships—past, present, and future. They shared stories of family grief and the holes in their hearts. They discussed war and peace, and I could feel my own tongue loosen as the buzz and euphoria overtook me. At times that night, I'm not even sure what I said. At one point Solomon came to check on me and said, "Never take a dolphin to a dog fight."

I eventually extricated myself from two women who'd been holding on to me while I spoke about my parents, the fluidity of my father, and the sparks of my mother. I found myself stationed at the swimming pool and gave myself the job of lifeguard. It felt more natural to watch over the animated coven. Solomon and Mona were nowhere to be seen. In the end, I became scared of falling in. I looked into the pool like a crystal ball and found myself thinking about a time Solomon and I hung out in a bar with our folks in between river cruises.

The *Aces* had been full of gamblers that trip and everyone was in a great mood. Solomon and I gathered cash from the adults and made trips to the bar for pitchers of beer after they seated everyone outside for making too much noise. We snuck a glass from each pitcher and were pretty wobbly by the end of the night. Uncle Miles, thief that he was, noticed that we had been pulling out drinks for ourselves and sold us out. Pops wasn't pissed until Miles muttered, "Damn kid can't take care of anything or anyone. What a waste."

Pops stood up, got him in a headlock, and started slamming his head against the table. The glasses and pitchers spilled until the surface was a dark river. Everyone scattered. They knew the drill. Cops would be called. They scurried to the shadows. All but my mother. She stared at me like I was to blame. Her face hardened with a familiar look, a combination of disappointment and anger. The unspoken subtext of my childhood: my mother hated me even though she mostly tried to hide it. Now, the swimming pool housed a creature from my past, a shape that not even the rising sun could disperse.

I finally wandered into the house and discovered several women huddled over a laptop on the coffee table. They were watching a video of animals attacking humans. They looked up at me, embarrassed, and scattered when I approached. Perhaps, their demons were as powerful as my own. I sat at on the couch and brought up another browser, checking to see if anyone had responded to my posting on Craigslist. The room smelled vaguely like burned hair and fresh-sliced oranges.

The reply to my posting was short and it could have been from anyone, I suppose. Only it wasn't: *L Hotel, Vegas*. It was from my folks. My goddamn Pops and my pissed-off Moms. They were alive.

8

SHADOW WHISPER

On Sunday, I slept for nearly a full day but felt more tired than ever when I woke for my first shift at Club Paradise. Outside, the sun was bleeding its arrival into the gray mass, the LA sky hanging over us like a giant lung. What combo of drugs had I taken? Solomon had loaned me a pair of black slacks and T-shirt, the unofficial uniform for security there. I showered and dressed in the bathroom, trying to make sense of everything that was happening. The door to his room was closed. He hadn't been particularly helpful on the topic of my parents being alive. All Solomon said as I drove him home after the Goddess Guides party was: "This is what your folks do—the make you feel responsible for their shit. My advice is to ditch them like they ditched you."

Why had Moms and Pops had faked their deaths in the first place? To trick their creditors? To pull a con? To lose the dead weight in their lives like me? The absorbed twin inside of me wanted me to drive to Vegas to confront them, but I knew that I needed to get my shit together first. The questions I had went deeper than why they were assholes.

There was no one on the street as I walked to Club Paradise. Very little differentiated early morning LA from a zombie apocalypse. I sensed a tiny figure following me but whenever I turned there was nothing but gray sidewalk and sky. Everything in Los Angeles was a shadow. I couldn't help but feel that something bad was flickering on the horizon. Was I a parasite in LA or a predator to be snuffed out like my pal Conrad had doled out to all matter of insects? I would soon be entering a world as dangerous as the army, and I didn't even know who I was.

Before long I found myself facing the closed doors of Club Paradise. It was nearly eight a.m., but I didn't want to bang on the faux castle entrance. I thought about hanging out in the misfit statue garden or sitting on the lip of the moat driveway. I was too on edge, though. A *thwapping* sound drew my attention. It appeared to be coming from behind the club. The brick driveway circled around until it splayed outward in concrete to form a surprisingly large back parking lot. There were a few cars here, mostly junkers. I wondered if they belonged to employees or drunks who'd cabbed home after throwing back a few too many. A warehouse directly behind the club had a faded red sign that read *Far Horizon*. This could be a name for anything: import/export, machine parts, women's underwear.

I cleared the corner of a building. A skinny boy on the verge of puberty, with black hair and light brown skin, was tossing a tennis ball against a metal garage door. The sound was louder now. CLANG. CLANG. CLANG. He wore a Yasiel Puig Dodgers jersey and fielded grounders with a worn leather glove and short steps that covered ground with almost supernatural quickness. Without warning, he speared a backhand, spun, and flung the tennis ball at my head. I held up a hand and snatched the ball before it could smack me in the forehead.

"Looks like you passed the first test," the kid said.

"Hold your jets there, Yoda. Who the hell are you?"

"I'm your boss."

"I met Biz Z and you're not him."

"Then I'm one of your bosses. My name is Iman Pourali," the kid said. "I'm Big Z's kid."

"Name's West and I'm here to—"

"Let me stop you right there, hired help. First of all, that Yoda shit pissed me off. I hate that Star Wars and Star Trek crap. I'm not a nerd you can sweet talk so put that shit back in your pants. Second, you have no idea what you're here to do. Third, your name seems as fake as the breasts of the skanks at the club."

"Is that right?" I asked, lobbing the ball back, trying to hide my surprise at the kid's language and how quickly he was sorting me out. "What kind of name's Iman Pourali anyway?"

"Iman in Persian means faith, like you gotta have it in me, hombre. And Pourali sounds just Italian enough so that me and my brother can get tail without letting the chicks know we're half Iranian and half Irish, or as we like to call ourselves Irishanians. Dad's hoping my brother Malik settles down with a Persian princess even though he himself went out of the tribe to get busy with my mom."

"You seriously want me to believe that you get tail?" I asked, and instantly regretted revving up this pint-sized chatterbox.

"Gentlemen don't kiss and tell. But I'm not a gentleman!"

"And you think I am?"

"I've got more game than you." As though to demonstrate, Iman hurled the ball against the garage door and turned his back to spear the tennis ball in a basket catch over his shoulder.

"Is that supposed to impress me?"

"No, but this will. Catch me if you can, slowpoke!" Iman yelled out as a challenge, his lanky legs instantly in motion. He sprinted toward an adjacent alley next to the loading bay. I launched myself in pursuit, careful to dodge the broken bottles and discarded trash. Iman showed no such restraint. The little dude churned up objects in his wake along the fenced-in parking lot next to an abandoned warehouse. The concrete plot was choked with weeds and machine parts that were too rusted or busted to steal. The concertina along the top reminded me of the motor pool in Bagram—the smell of piss and cigarette butts was like GI perfume. Perhaps I'd not traveled as far as I had originally thought. At the end of the alley, the kid stopped short of the sidewalk and yelled, "Iman gets the gold and West gets the silver!"

I caught up after a few more strides and doubled over, trying to control my breathing. How could I already be this out of shape? Civilian life was more dangerous to returning GIs than war. Boredom, booze, and bad decisions pulled soldiers into the drain of America, where they clogged the streets like discarded pubic hair and soap scum.

Iman waved me over to an immense stand-alone garage. The structure seemed misplaced in the alleyway, with an exterior that you would expect to see connected to a mansion. Did there use to be a house standing next to it? Two cameras slanted down from the roof, and Iman buzzed an intercom before flipping the bird to both lenses. A woman's voice squawked on the speaker, "You better not let your father see you do that!"

"Everyone knows you wear the pants. Are you going to open up or what?" Iman asked.

The door slid open and the lights flicked on. The walls were painted the color of lime slices stuffed into Coronas in summertime. We stepped inside and the doors slid behind us, making me feel instantly claustrophobic. Two highly polished black town cars were housed in the four-car garage, next to a carport holding skis, tennis rackets, and golf equipment. A third car, a later model silver Mercedes, gleamed from a recent wax job. A woman waited for us impatiently, but it wasn't Iman's mother. It couldn't be. For starters she was around eighteen, leaning against a closed steel door. She had hazel skin, almond-shaped brown eyes with flecks of gold, and light brown hair pulled back in a ponytail. She wore a smirk and was dressed in black yoga pants and a tube top, both too tight and displaying a muscular body with curves that made it difficult to look away.

I couldn't help but stammer, finally spitting out: "I'm…"

"Late!" the young woman finished my sentence with a confident tone, part impatience, part sarcasm, part humor, difficult to read.

"Put your eyes back into your head, West! That's my sister," Iman said.

"I see you've met my daughter," the woman's voice on the intercom stated matter-of-factly. Her name is Nikki and mine is Bianca."

"Please to meet you both," I said.

"What a suck-up," Iman said.

"West, welcome to our employ. Currently, Deacon, Flynn, and you are responsible for security at Club Paradise. I'm not sure if you've noticed, but the club also is connected to the Pourali family residence. My home is a place you will never see and is only accessible from this garage and a series of secure steel doors from the club. These two worlds do not and *will not* coexist. Do you understand?"

"Roger," I said. I knew a little something about keeping personal and professional lives separate. While on leave, I'd refused to answer any questions from Deirdre or Solomon about the prisoners I'd guarded in Afghanistan or the war in general. I understood a mother's desire to separate sin from the day-to-day workings of her family.

"Good," Bianca continued. "I will set your schedule. In general, you'll be on the night shift, except when I need you to give Deacon a day off, which he has today. Iman is my eyes and ears."

"I'm a lot more than that," Iman complained. "I'm the brains."

"No, you're not," Nikki said in a bored, superior tone that reminded me of Deirdre.

"Iman will provide you with your schedule, your pay, and instructions that you will follow to the letter. I want to be very clear. Your job is to support the club and the Pourali family, but you work for me...and only me. Do you understand, Buddy?"

There it was—my real name. Somehow, Bianca had found out about my past and obviously wasn't fucking around. It was also clear that if I didn't watch my step, I could be turned in to the authorities. I wondered if they had something on the other club staff. There was so much that I didn't understand and yet I managed to spit out, "I understand."

"Jesus, he's slow," Iman said. "Mom, are you sure we want him working for us?"

"I'm sure. Iman, go see your father at the coffee shop and give him *his* list. West, you're now running late getting Nikki to her job."

"I'm on it," I said as Nikki pressed the keys into my palm and gestured at the rear of the car with a flip of her ponytail. I tiptoed around and opened the door trying not to stare at her backside as she climbed inside. I shut the door to say goodbye to the pipsqueak, but Iman had already bolted off down the alley. They wanted me to be a chauffeur? Okay, so be it. I climbed in and adjusted the seat and side mirrors. There was a new car smell in the immaculate town car and the windows were tinted. I put the car keys in the ignition and a small pink note dropped to the floor. *THE CAR IS BUGGED*, was scrawled in block letters. Why would someone be listening in to a conversation between a teenager and her driver? I pocketed the note and started the car, backing out into the lot slowly, the garage door closing behind me automatically.

I was still groggy and trying to be careful, driving cautiously enough so that Nikki complained, "West, you ARE slow. And my brother is almost never right. Can you step on it?"

"Where to?"

"Punch 'Hair Empire' into our GPS and try not to go over any bumps. I have to put on my face."

After a few minutes, I figured out how to program the GPS. Hair Empire was only a mile away. This new world seemed insular in such a sprawling metropolis. Nikki painted shadows around her eyes with a short brush as I inched into the street. I really didn't feel like getting canned on my first day by smudging Nikki's eyeliner.

"I don't understand how that garage connects with the main building," I said.

"There's a lot you don't understand," she said. "Some Hollywood mogul built a tunnel, a bomb shelter, a bowling alley, and a movie theater below the castle. Only my parents would turn that monstrosity into a strip club and a home. I use both phrases loosely."

The sarcasm was tangible, but beneath it was pain and frustration. I waited until I saw the brush drop back into Nikki's purse before accelerating into traffic. In the rearview, she smiled and blew me a kiss, and I fixed my eyes forward, not without feeling dread that a crash of another kind was inevitable.

I saw more death in the waiting area of Hair Empire than I had witnessed on even the worst day in Afghanistan. It was not a hair salon. It was a lice removal business on the second floor of a dingy mini mall. There was no adequate explanation for what took place in that square room of death. It was a slaughterhouse of lice, plain and simple, a spectacle that my exterminator pal Conrad would have appreciated. It reminded me of cracking open crawfish for Moms after Pops boiled them, an activity that I'd despised with a passion. Was that why they'd let me think they were dead for so long…to toughen me up?

I was immediately given the once-over by Donya, Big Z's older sister, with intense brown eyes and muscular hands, hair covered with a scarf. She shooed me over to the waiting area like a stray dog and waved her muscular arm at her niece. Nikki complied by shuffling over to a station between two Latinas. They were spritzing down the seats with a foamy green liquid from plastic spray bottles and homemade labels they hawked in a front counter display. Nikki did not look at her aunt directly and I could sense an undercurrent of tension. There was certainly no slack given for family members here. Minutes mattered. Donya closely supervised every aspect of the delousing, even after the doors opened to a steady stream of customers.

The women worked with assembly line speed, brushing out the hair of children and their parents. None of the customers were happy, much like in a dentist's office, and I could see why. Their scalps were scraped and hair was pulled back to reveal the parasites. I leaned forward in my seat to make sure that my hair didn't touch anything, even by chance, and I started to itch from head to toe. I had, more than once as a kid, had lice, which my mother treated with a painful home remedy that included kerosene and camphor before shaving me bald.

The clicking of ticks being crushed between the fingernails of the attendants was making me sick to my stomach. The appointments were steady all through the morning, and I managed to kill some time finishing my novel before I was left with a choice of observing the death squad or reading health and glamour magazines.

Finally, Donya had mercy on me for staying in my post. She winked at me and handed me a lunch order, written in what I assumed was Persian, along with the name and address of a restaurant called Kafir. I punched the directions into the town car's GPS but decided to hoof it after finding out that it was a few blocks away. I found myself navigating streets that alternated between Persian and Hebrew characters. Someone would later tell me that this area was called Tehrangeles, and that it was one of the largest populations of Iranians outside of the country. Many were refugees from the Shah's displacement, and some had come over with their wealth intact. I wandered past a bustling stretch of nail salons, small grocery stores, cafés, and an ice cream parlor with flavors like saffron, rose petal, and sage.

I dropped off the food order at Kafir, a tiny restaurant with signs in three languages. Next door, I ducked into a used bookstore, where a kid my own age had separated the stacks between Persian books and American paperbacks for the college students at UCLA just down the road. He was kind enough to trade in *The Green Ripper* for *The Girl in the Plain Brown Wrapper*—another Travis McGee mystery. The photo of the striking woman on the cover made me think about Nikki. She was a presence I couldn't escape.

My eyes were too tired to focus the rest of the afternoon and I passed into the world of daydreams, the monotony of hair-picking sending me into a trance. The feeling of waiting was familiar in a lifetime of waiting. I found myself thinking back to the first of a string of apartment complexes I'd lived in as a kid. One was on the outskirts of Lake Charles, next to a pond where I caught frogs and messed around with my friends. Solomon was always there in my early memories, but I sometimes dreamed about a girl, barely old enough to walk, who followed after us until one day she was gone. I couldn't remember her name, but for some reason, she reminded me of Nikki. I couldn't shake the feeling that I had somehow let this girl down. I occasionally caught a glimpse of her in the periphery of my vision when I was awake. But she wasn't there when I turned my head. Perhaps she had never been there.

I'd watched over destructive parents, headstrong friends like Solomon, dramatic women like Deirdre, and suffering prisoners of war. I cast myself as a protector without understanding why I felt the compulsion. There was some sense of loss always there just in the shadows, behind my back, outside of my reach, and I couldn't shake the feeling that I was responsible in some way for the family curse and my place in it.

At four o'clock, Nikki nudged my shoulder and I tried to shake off my daydreams. She gestured toward the door and I went to open it for her. I waved at Donya and the tired women cleaning up their stations. Passing close to Nikki's perfume, I caught a scent of vanilla, lavender, and something else familiar, from some past life, perhaps. As she passed, she whispered something that would change my life, two simple words in a barely audible whisper: "*Help me.*"

9

SHADOW CARDS

Help me. The plea echoed in my head for days, even while I was on security detail at Club Paradise. Sometimes I heard Nikki's voice, husky and needful. At other times, it was Solomon's voice, but mixed with the music at the club, the wall of sound he lived in to keep me from prying into his life of drugs and women. At other times, it was my own voice, the one that barked at me to hightail it back to Louisiana, return to the army and face my punishment. I attributed the voice to my dead twin inside me. My parents' voices were silent, of course. I wondered if they even wanted to see me again. Then there was a voice that bubbled from the cocktails and gray clouds, a tiny insistent cry like a small girl in the netherworld, or an underwater angel. I felt as empty as the kegs I wheeled out back for Flynn during my shifts. Even scaring the perverts from groping dancers and listening to the film-talk of the regulars didn't do anything to distract me.

Solomon thought I was out of my mind for stressing about Big Z's daughter. His take was that she was a rich girl looking to "pot the stir" which I assumed meant "stir the pot." He thought I should look out for myself. Be selfish. Reboot. Or else face the past and come to terms with my folks and the army. Nothing was worse to him than stasis, which is why he was always bouncing from one disaster to another.

I tried to distract myself by reading, but the voice of detective Travis McGee and his quest to save everyone around him brought me back to worrying about Nikki. Maybe she really was being held prisoner or being abused. I talked about it with Tarzana until she grew tired of the subject and stared off into space, twirling the blond curl on her index finger like spaghetti on a fork. I felt like I was going mad. I was cycling, folding into myself, waiting for a sign, and on Tuesday night I got one.

I was working security solo and Club Paradise was a tomb, even with happy hour extended to eight o'clock. I was doing little more than scowling at people flashing their IDs and listening to the dancers share war stories while I made my rounds. Beneath the costumes and makeup, the women on stage were fighting for their lives. They had tales of heartache, abandonment, abuse, financial turmoil, addiction to bad men, bad drugs, and bad scenes. I tried not to eavesdrop but couldn't help it. There had to be a pecking order among them, a dancer with knowledge of the inner workings of the club and the family who owned it. Someone who could get me closer to Nikki.

In the back of the strip club, one woman held court in the farthest corner opposite the bar. Her stage name was Alice, and she was the dancer I'd seen on stage on my first visit to Paradise. She was trying to pull off the innocence of a girl tumbling into the rabbit hole even though she was on the wrong side of thirty. Alice was a magnet to the other strippers. All of them circled around to talk to her at some point in the evening. At first, I wondered if I was imagining things. That is, until Big Z himself made an appearance on the balcony overhead and made a beeline to her. Everyone, staff and customers alike, paid attention when the former wrestler entered the floor. Whatever he had in mind wasn't for the masses. He approached with purpose, gripped Alice's elbow, and whispered in her ear. Their body language wasn't that of lovers, but still intimate, brother and sister, king and queen of Club Paradise.

I'd already heard plenty of rumors about Big Z. He once beat Lou Ferrigno in an arm-wrestling match. He could down a bottle of whiskey without showing signs of being drunk. He bedded each new dancer as a test and was rumored to have a fetish for having his toes sucked. And this was a man who wasn't exactly the type to get a mani-pedi. Some of the dancers refused to talk at all about him. Maybe it was just too weird or they were ashamed of what they'd done to get a gig. I was pissed that Big Z would use his position to entice the dancers to sleep with him. Between the stream of dancers visiting his office and Nikki's hint, I was starting to feel the urge to pop the ex-wrestler in the nose. It probably wouldn't do anything to anyone except land me in the hospital or jail.

I waited until Big Z left Alice's side and circled back to the bar to make my move. All the regulars were there, and the club owner slid in next to Flynn, holding court, chatting up the clientele. I made a circuit around the main stage looking over the customers the way Deacon had shown me. I puffed out my chest and swung my arms like a simian, taking up space. I was supposed to remind them that paradise was earned by following the rules and spending money at a regular rate. I eyed anyone nursing beers or holding on to their wallets. The women, of course, followed the greenback in concentric circles. The only problem was that there were too many women and too few men. How was Club Paradise able to afford so much staff and square footage? There was something to the puzzle I was missing. Meanwhile, Big Z played jovial host and mixed drinks.

"Hi there," I said, heading over to Alice. She pocketed her cell phone and gave me the once-over. Her washed-out blue eyes were framed by blond hair showing dark roots from a dye job too far in the past. The bow of her little girl dress spooled behind her like tiny wings. The rules of what passed for fashion in the darkness were different from those in the light.

"Hi there," she said, low and serious, in a mock effort to mimic my voice. "I'm Alice Winter or as I like to say Alice in Winterland."

"Cute."

"Winter's cold. Not cute."

"I'm West."

"No last name?" she asked.

"No first name," I shot back.

"You're the one who's cute. Maybe I should adopt you," she said, and I couldn't help but think of my miserable relationship with my folks.

"Not sure what kind of mom you'd be," I said, and her face froze, suddenly more serious.

"Can I give you some advice?"

"You can give it. I'm immune to common sense."

"I hope not," Alice said. "Get out of this hellhole while you can. I've been watching you. You think you can just observe everyone and not get involved. Once those damn blinds close, this club only has one exit: down, into depravity, dread, despair."

"That's a lot of D-words."

"Yep, the devil likes them. This place is for the cursed."

I wasn't spooked exactly but Alice was starting to get under my skin. I felt drawn to her like some shadow sister in a cash-only world. Her smile held the promise of something sparkly lost long ago even as her eyes carried a pang of sadness. Neither of us spoke for a few moments until I heard a Big Z's voice behind me. He'd snuck up while my attention was on Alice and Solomon was pumping up the house music for each stripper's five minutes on stage.

"I need you to do something for me," Big Z said.

"Yes, boss."

"My cousin Yar is in the back room."

"I didn't see him come in."

"Service entrance," Big Z said. "Sometimes I like to do business not out in the open."

"Understood," I said.

"Good." He brushed his index finger above his lip as though he had a mustache. "Yar's been beating me at poker and generally annoying me. I want you to intimidate him and get him the hell out of my place before I fuck him up."

"Can't you ask him to leave?"

"And be rude to family? Never."

"I'll take care of it," I said, and tried to ignore Alice sticking out her tongue behind the former wrestler's back in a bizarre effort to make me laugh.

I followed several steps behind Big Z. He marched past a

placard displaying the health inspector's B restaurant rating. The sign had been defaced by a red marker—two nipples had been added to the loops of the letter rating. I wondered if a drunk customer or a bored employee was to blame. We shouldered our way through swinging kitchen doors and padded across industrial black rubber mats stretched across the concrete floor. We marched past sizzling burners, wafting tacos, french fries, and lively conversation in Spanish between the line cook and dishwasher.

We passed the back service entrance, now closed, next to a walk-in cooler. It was stocked with an impressive amount of mostly domestic beer and liquor that I suspected was watered down at the bar well. The door to Big Z's office was open and he gestured for me to follow him inside. The layout was straight from the 1960s with oak paneling, a stocked mini-bar, an almost life-sized framed photo of himself in a shirtless wresting pose, and a mahogany desk in the far corner next to a bolted door that supposedly led to his private upstairs apartment—Big Z's home away from home. There was a small window like that of a prison at eye level, overlooking the faded sign on the building across the street: *Far Horizon.*

There was a circular table in the center of the room with a worn felt surface being used for poker. Even the card game was old school, five-card draw instead of Texas hold 'em, with three men of various ages gripping cards. The youngest card player was my age. I immediately pegged him for Malik, Big Z's eldest son, on resemblance alone as he was an incredible physical specimen in his own right. The second man was midthirties, wore a rumpled black suit, and was Asian, Thai, or Filipino perhaps, with a predator's gaze. I assumed that he was the muscle for the last man at the table—a tall, thin dude of Middle Eastern descent, in white Converse tennis shoes and an expensive navy-blue Italian suit. This must be Yar.

"So, this is the new bouncer?" Malik asked in a sarcastic tone that reminded me of his brother.

"Doesn't seem very impressive," the Asian bodyguard said. Big Z ignored the barbs. "West, this is my eldest son Malik, my cousin Yar, and his associate Mitzu."

I nodded to the players at the table, each in turn. Big Z settled into his chair and picked up his cards with a sigh. No wonder he was losing. Without taking my eyes off Mitzu, I circled around the table and stopped at the inset bar directly behind Yar. This got his attention. If looks could kill, I would have been a dark stain on the floor. This dude had a bad attitude and temper, and Solomon was playing with fire by sleeping with his wife.

"So, this is your play now, cuz?" Yar asked in a brash, impolite tone.

"I'm sorry, cousin. Not sure I understand."

"You hate losing. You always have. So, you decide to come back with your lackey to signal what's in my hand."

"That's ridiculous," Big Z said. "I've told you that drugs make you paranoid."

"Family makes me paranoid," Yar said. "I remember your father was a bastard."

"As was yours."

"At least my bodyguard is in the game. How the hell am I supposed to trust you in our business together?"

Big Z didn't dignify this with a response. With the precision of a knife stroke from a practiced chef, he flicked his gaze at me and returned it to his cards. I took this as my cue.

"Yar, I've noticed that your bodyguard has very few chips and you have the most," I said.

"Maybe I'm a much better player," Yar said.

"It's much more likely that you've worked out signals with Mitzu in order to increase your odds," I said.

"I didn't ask for your opinion." Yar shot me a sidelong glance over his shoulder. "What do you know about poker anyway?"

"Almost everything there is. For example, you spoke about trust. You're playing in Big Z's place and you're winning. That alone should make you trust him," I said.

"How do you figure?"

"He could easily have this room decked out with cameras, with a light that flashes when he should bet. It's an easy setup. Not sure if you noticed, but Big Z has cameras everywhere in Club Paradise. He's just not using them to fuck you. Unlike the scam you're pulling with your associate here."

I nodded at Mitzu. The dude lurched halfway to his feet, all muscle, tattoos, and testosterone. A single disapproving look by Yar stopped him mid-rise. Mitzu reluctantly settled back into his chair, gripping his cards with two hands like he was going to rip them in half. I should have been scared, I suppose, but I didn't feel anything at all. Yar stood, but I didn't move back from my spot, even as he turned toward me, our faces inches apart.

"You've insulted me," Yar said.

"Sorry," I said.

"Not accepted."

"How about I give you one free shot at my head? I promise I won't block you."

Yar smiled as though I was off the hook just before clenching his right fist and driving it toward my face. His long wind-up gave me time to duck my head so that his fist hit the top of my skull. I heard a crack of his knuckles and my legs felt rubbery. Yar yelped in pain, gripping his hand.

"You'll pay for this," Mitzu said, hands dipping into his jacket pocket for emphasis.

"For what? I didn't block him. I kept my part of the bargain."

Big Z beamed a wide smile at his cousin. Yar clenched his teeth in response before tossing his cards into the pot and stomping out the door, clutching his fist.

"What's the matter, have a bad hand?" Big Z asked.

Mitzu shook his head and followed his boss out the door. I tried to look nonchalant even though my head rang from the blow. I felt the top of my head; it was bleeding, probably from one of Yar's rings. I barely tracked Malik getting to his feet and slapping me on the back. "This one's got balls."

"Even better he follows orders," Big Z said. "And he knows how to make a statement."

Big Z reached into the breast pocket of his blazer, peeled a hundred-dollar bill off a wad held by a gold money clip, and slipped it into my front pants pocket. It was a practiced gesture from a man with experience stuffing bills into strange places. I tried to ignore the eyes of both my boss and his son, but I felt dirty in ways that I couldn't explain.

I stumbled out of Big Z's office and found myself in a stupor. When I arrived back at the club, I paced around the inner perimeter, like I was back in the army doing my rounds. Counting prisoners. Dancers: check. Regulars: check. Solomon: absent. Looks like he'd loaded a playlist and bailed. He probably was out in the parking lot, getting high. I thought I saw a small shadow dart into the women's dressing room. Could one of the women have brought along one of their kids? Ridiculous. I was seeing things again.

Outside, I breathed deeply in and out, and then followed the brick moat around to the back of the club. Cars dotted the parking lot. Malik and Solomon were there, sharing a cigarette behind the loading dock. Malik sneered and cuffed Solomon on the back of the head before racing down the alley to catch up with Yar and Mitzu who'd stopped at the fence to the Far Horizon warehouse. Solomon shuffled over to me while the three men unlocked the gate and disappeared inside the building. Lights flickered on and the window lit up in different parts of the building like spider eyes.

Solomon offered me a drag off his smoke. It was barely more than a butt.

I shook my head. "Not looking to start another bad habit."

"You pissed off Yar tonight. Malik told me," Solomon said.

"Just doing my job."

"Stop that shit if you can help it. I don't want you or I to get on his bad side. Especially since Mona's his wife."

"This family's trouble," I muttered. "You should quit messing around with her."

"No Sherlock, shit," he said. The tone was meant to be light but I could see that we were in over our heads. Eventually, I would find a way to protect him like I'd been unable to do with the prisoners back in Afghanistan. My knees felt weak. The air was thick with car exhaust. The top of my head was still bleeding. Looked like I'd have another scar, this one hidden, though. Not nearly enough penance for the failure I'd become.

10

SHADOW PROJECTION

You should strut around like your theme song is playing. Life's a movie and you're the star. This was one of the tidbits of sage advice from Pops, not his worst by any stretch. To be clear, Pops tried to teach me to be tough and to scrap for what I wanted. With Moms, it was more that she didn't recognize motherhood to be an actual thing. She'd always treated me like a houseguest, some unwanted relative she couldn't shake off. They'd always pushed me to be self-sufficient, and between the two of them, I had plenty of chances to revel in my independence, a path that had led me to the order of the military and now back into disorder. I wasn't sure what I'd learned along the way, wasn't sure who I was supposed to be.

This new city confused me at every turn. The river in Los Angeles was a cruel joke. It spooled like an artery through the city's concrete skin and barely could muster enough water to reach the sea. Solomon took me to see it one night after he woke me up from one of his Goddess Guide gigs. He was talkative and made me drive him downtown and park beneath a bridge. We slipped through a hole in a chain-link fence and sat on the embankment. He was in a bad mood, worked up about something. We sipped beers and watched the sun come up over the water, such that it was, a trickle really.

"Something bad's going to happen, Buddy," Solomon told me after a long silence.

"Why is that exactly?"

"Because something bad is always going to happen."

"That's why I'm here."

"No offense. You can't take care of your damn self."

"Never said I could. I'm here to watch out for you."

"You're here because you're lost, bro'. I'm nothing but trouble. You know that."

"True. If it's not the women, it's the drugs," I said.

"It's both this time."

"We should bail. Get the hell out of LA tonight."

"What's wrong with us is something we can't run from. You know that better than anyone."

Solomon stared at the rivulet like he missed Old Man River. Our childhood was filled with currents scraping over primordial ooze, the legends of monster catfish and river creatures, the siren song to New Orleans. Solomon always had a plan and I was his bodyguard, keeping him out of scrapes with older boys and the law. At times, he was his own worst enemy. I was there, of course, the time we ran away from home and constructed our own raft from kite string, bungee cords, and warped lumber from an abandoned construction site. We talked smack and hitched elaborate knots, channeling our inner Huck and Tom. Of course, we sank almost instantly and lost my Batman watch, Solomon's cowboy hat, a canteen, an apple pie baked by Solomon's mom (this is what landed us the spankings), and a deck of cards with nudie pictures I borrowed from Uncle Miles. Even though we came back around sunset, clothes still damp from the plunge, I don't think anyone would have noticed we'd taken off if it hadn't been for that damn pie.

Solomon's mother, Beatrice, aside from being a helluva baker, lived the life of an artist, with a revolving door of men and the need to roll a joint before her feet touched the floor. Solomon once snuck me into his mom's bedroom and showed me the tray of green buds and rolling papers underneath her bed. He would occasionally pilfer her stash to try to score with some girl or to make a couple bucks when he needed it. Beatrice played the piano on the *Aces* riverboat. Her love of music was one of the few things she shared with Solomon. "He can play anything...and anyone," she liked to brag. After *Aces* suffered structural damage from the hurricane, Beatrice started giving music lessons and Solomon became claustrophobic with his mom underfoot. Solomon didn't stay around long in Lake Charles after the funerals of my folks. He threw his few possessions (most of them records) into his gold Impala and took off for the Big Easy.

At first, Solomon scraped by as a busboy in a tourist restaurant, before catching a break to DJ in a dance club La Boucherie (which was French for meat market). I visited him almost every weekend with and without Deirdre, and we drank ourselves into sunsets. Just like tonight. I felt like there was something he wasn't telling me but maybe I was paranoid. One thing for certain—I was going to be keeping an eye on him.

Club Paradise was starting to feel like home and that worried me. I found myself hanging out in the nook between the bar and kitchen, the best vantage to keep an eye on the dancers and Solomon. I hadn't been asked to drive Nikki in a couple of days, but Deacon took off at one point to take her to a movie. I wondered when I would see her again. Alice surprised me by moving over to an open barstool and discussing the film the regulars were shooting. From what I could tell she was involved in the production. Blake occasionally brushed his hand on her shoulder and she didn't seem freaked out by it.

Solomon disappeared into the girl's locker room and all the dancers followed him inside. Deacon announced a slight break in the action, and one of the men took the initiative to head to the bar to grab drinks. Tarzana was the first to emerge from the women's locker room. Solomon stumbled out after her and returned to the DJ booth to put on her songs for her set. Alice returned to her table in the corner and the other dancers filtered out of the locker room to hang with the male clientele. On stage, Tarzana looked zoned out and didn't pay attention to the guys flinging money at her. When she was done, Alice had to collect the bills for her and tuck them inside her leopard-skin bikini bottoms. I was so engrossed with the show after the show that I didn't notice Big Z making his entrance into the main room. He must have come from the staircase or some other entrance. The ex-wrestler looked pissed off, all business. He nodded at Alice and headed back to his back office.

Tarzana and Alice exchanged whispers. I was headed over to ask them what the hell was going on, but before I reached them, Tarzana flung herself toward the back office. The door slammed behind her, and Alice shook her head, slipping back to her table. Just another night of weirdness in the club and there was no one to talk to about it, no one I could trust other than Solomon, who'd disappeared. Maybe he was out back smoking. I was so tired and spacey that I didn't even feel like reading the new detective novel I'd scored. Hours slowly ticked away, much in the way they had in the army. Day finally gave way to night and the blinds whirred shut. The darkness of the club solidified into something more than just banks of shadows holding form against the track lighting and the sneers of totems from the walls. There was something sordid and sentient in the architecture of the club itself. How long would I ferment in this soup of sweat and booze before I was ready to take the next step forward in my life?

I idled in the town car outside of the Sunset Valley Theater, an old-style movie theater that played second-run films. Tonight's feature was Tootsie, a movie I hadn't seen in years, one that Pops had appreciated for the long con. Of course, you had to have commitment to pull off a scam like that. Sometimes out-of-the-box thinking could pay big dividends. When I'd reminded him that Tootsie nearly lost everything from the lies, he thought that was bullshit. Hollywood got the happy ending wrong. Tootsie should have kept the scam going until there was enough bank to retire.

Malik stewed next to me and hadn't spoken a word since he convinced me to pull into the loading zone. The dude was obviously in a bad mood, that much was clear when he yanked me from the club to drive him to the theater. He scanned the front entrance like a sniper, waiting for the show to let out. When he saw the first trickle of customers leave, he jumped out of the passenger seat, ignored the ticket booth, and rushed the door, shouldering his way in behind a man exiting through the swinging doors. It was a bit blurry behind the glass but I thought I saw Malik shove a skinny white kid on his ass right in front of Nikki. He grabbed his sister's wrist and led her out the front door. Both waged an epic battle of swearing with Nikki holding her own.

They got in the back seat, and I wasn't about to wait around for cops. I pulled out in front of a bus and onto Wilshire and set the GPS for Club Paradise.

"What the hell did you just do, Malik?"

"Helping you out, sis. You know that asshole Doug was on Dad's banned list."

"I can make my own choices, dumbass! I'm nineteen."

"You live under Dad's roof. He pays your college and you have to follow his rules."

"Like you do? Don't think I don't know about some of the shit you do behind his back?"

"That's different," Malik said.

"Because you're a boy?"

"Yes, goddammit."

"Do you think it's a coincidence that Dad owns a strip club? He's a monster."

"Who buys you whatever you want," Malik said.

"He preys on women. In the club. Mom. Me. You have no clue."

"Shut up about Dad! Or I'll fucking rat you out," Malik said.

Brother and sister stared out the windows, motionless as statues. I navigated the course home. I found myself thinking about Tarzana and the other strippers Big Z took up into his apartment. Was Nikki a victim too? I was getting sucked into the family drama; I couldn't help myself. The only role I knew in life was to play protector, something I'd failed at time and time again, but eventually, I would succeed. Eventually, like the hapless detective Travis McGee, my sacrifice would mean something to someone.

Later that night I was in a dark mood. Flynn noticed and drifted over, trying to make small talk about his movie. When he saw I was out of it he poured me a cup of black coffee and told me to head up to the tower at the end of my shift. There I'd find spare lights to replace the burned-out bulbs hanging intermittently throughout all levels of the club. The tower was accessible by a winding staircase beside the VIP room. It was the only place, other than the girls' changing room and the two-bedroom apartment above Big Z's office, that I hadn't yet been.

Solomon didn't return the rest of the night. He'd have a bead on the dynamics at the club and help me get my bearings. Maybe Nikki was being held hostage by an abusive father. Most likely, I'd already gotten myself into something I shouldn't have; the real problem was how much I was drawn to danger in all of its forms. Pops had always told me that I was more at home on the gambling riverboat than anywhere else, poking around in the nooks and crannies of the vessel, making friends with the employees, and skimming desserts from the kitchen. In the end, it was a floating prison but one that I had replicated with a real one in the army, and again, now, with writhing women with nowhere else to go, just like myself, living in a ghost existence off the grid.

My head throbbed and I stayed on the periphery of the club, circling around the outskirts along the wall totems. I tracked a couple of the strippers wandering off to remote corners of the establishment for their lap dances. I occasionally needed to threaten a joker that was too handsy but could do little for the women who disappeared to meet one of the men out in the parking lot, for under-the-table dealings that I was advised to only loosely monitor. This made the grounds, front and back, part of my circuit. Once an hour I weaved in and among the smokers, the drug takers, and the occasional car in the back lot with the hair of one of the dancers bobbing in the moonlight beside another satisfied customer.

The behavior was reckless and put the club at risk, but Flynn had pulled me aside and let me know that the cops weren't a problem for us unless someone got hurt. This gave me an extra reason to keep my eyes and ears peeled and to question everything. Tarzana did not emerge from Big Z's office, and I found myself wondering what kind of creep I was working for.

By the time Flynn rang the bell for *last call*, I was starting to come out of my stupor. The lights flicked off and on, and the girls disappeared into the dressing room. I ushered a few stragglers out the door and the dancers followed behind them minutes later, half of them in costume, half dressed in sweats and jeans with streaked mascara. The regulars followed Flynn to a broom closet next to the DJ station. The bartender unlocked the door and they pulled out a digital camera and recording equipment. They headed to the basement door wedged between the bar and kitchen entrance, and disappeared into the bowels of the building.

Meanwhile, I worked on shutting down the place, making sure there weren't any guests hiding out on the premises. I wasn't sure what to make of Flynn and the regulars down in the basement after hours shooting their film. Curiosity overpowered my tiredness. The only dancer left was Alice, who opened the basement door with a small key around her neck. She bent over in her short skirt as though the eyes of men were still on her, and I suppose they were. At least one. She disappeared downstairs and I double-checked the women's dressing room and the bathrooms before locking the front door and using my own key to follow her downstairs.

The stairs were oddly designed, a single corkscrew metallic spiral leading upward to the west tower and downward to a double-wide hallway flanked by doors on either side, running the width of the building. There were a dozen rooms in all, of different shapes, and these had been used as film sets, according to Flynn, for nearly forty years. At the end of the hallway were two metallic doors propped open with cinderblocks and leading to a large open room filled with props, a makeup mirror, and a circular table. A tiny voice in my head propelled me, and I couldn't help but think that it was the voice of my family curse, pulling me forward. Alice reclined in front of the mirror, with Judd drawing additional layers of black makeup onto her face. It made her look somewhere between ghostlike and demonic.

Irv and Salt huddled up at the table, making notes on the shooting script of *Sirens*, and Flynn looked like he wanted to kill everyone in the room. Spokane stared at Alice's reflection in the mirror. This prompted his producer girlfriend, Salt, to slap him gently across the face. Spokane didn't move in response. Instead, he reached into his shirt pocket and dry swallowed a couple of white capsules. I'd stopped at the edge of the room, half in light, half in shadows.

"You're ex-military, aren't you?" a voice whispered behind a stack of lighting equipment in a slight alcove off the hallway. Blake stepped out with earphones dangling around his neck and a boom mike that he wielded like a lightsaber or a sword.

"You're ex-NSA, aren't you?" I whispered back.

"Guilty," he conceded. "Guilty for the rest of my fucking life." The slur in his voice was obvious now and he pulled me over to the side of the doorway. "You're like me, man. You sit on the sidelines and observe. The only difference is I've learned to use my skills to get what I want. Take that hottie in the make-up chair."

"Alice," I said stiffly.

"B-I-N-G-O," he spelled out. "She's kind of my girlfriend."

"I kind of think this isn't my business," I said.

"What's your story, West? What did you do to end up here?"

"Just about everything. Not that it's any of your business."

"Jesus, I can't tell sometimes in this city. You like girls, though, right?"

"I like women."

"Then you know what I mean. Everyone's trying to get into Alice's pants. Sometimes I even think Salt is. Let me tell you what's going on here."

Blake pulled the headset over his ears and pointed the end of the microphone at Alice. "You see Alice is playing two characters. One good, and the other a siren, her evil half, whispering dangerous things into the ears of the people who give her trouble in her life. Her dark half gets revenge, even when she doesn't really want it. This fucks her up. She's practicing lines with that artist. I call him Judo Judd because nothing you ever say seems to stick with that kid. He's talented, though. He's delivering dialogue better than most of the actors in this town, but it all hurts my ears if you know what I mean?"

"You don't have to involve me in your eavesdropping. I'm good."

"The hell you are," Blake snorted. "That act doesn't fool me. Flynn wants Spokane to stick to the script and his sugar mama producer won't have any of it. She's editing the damn thing, and everyone is pissed off. Irv acts like he's some big shot on the set of a hundred-million-dollar flick. He's bored of getting lap dances and casting himself in the role of the siren's boyfriend. Deacon couldn't believe he was cut out of the script. Everyone's talking and no one's listening," Blake concluded with a self-satisfied smirk.

It was hard to track the dynamics of the strange group congregating below ground, fueled by the ghosts of Hollywood's past, present, and future. I turned to walk away, noticing the dead bulbs in the hallway and my promise earlier that evening to Flynn to replace them. The lights, apparently, weren't the only things burned out here. I held two fingers up to my temple in a half-assed salute and walked away from the strange congregation looking to shoot through the night. As I marched away, I glanced over my shoulder and noticed that Blake's microphone had not been plugged in. Crazy dude. Everyone here was involved in some slow-boiling tragedy. This was a place for the damned, and I felt right at home.

Pops was occasionally a philosophical man. His pontifications erupted in the middle of the night when he'd wander over drunk to my travel cot in some corner of a crowded room and shake me awake. He also tended to repeat himself. One of his favorite rants was about how human nature had its winners and losers, and a third species, the losers that fed on the other losers—the parasites. Because there would always be many more losers than winners, and then those who hid in the darkness, feeding on misery to sustain themselves, would find a way to survive, if not thrive.

I never saw eye-to-eye with my folks on many things. They never set rules for me and the rules didn't apply to them either. It drove them crazy, I know, to have a kid enamored with doing the right thing. They would have hated my decision to join the military but would have totally understood my AWOL exodus to live in the shadows. Perhaps, the curse was a real thing, more powerful than intentions, a combination of family character flaws, ill timing, and awful luck.

I sat cross-legged in the tower above the strip club, breathing in and out as I'd learned to do in martial arts, trying to get some balance back in my world. I'd climbed the steps to the tower a dozen times already, departing with one bulb, and wandering the corridors of the club to illuminate the shadows. The shuttered windows made me feel claustrophobic like a fairy-tale princess who'd been awful to her parents.

I stood up and shook off the tingling in my legs. I felt tired but oddly refreshed. Sunrise pinked the sky over the tower on the residential side of Club Paradise. As with the transition to nighttime, the metal coverings over the window lifted. The Hollywood producer who'd built the place had a strange sense of humor or else had early plans to hide what bumped in the night behind these faux castle walls. In the east tower, a light flicked on, illuminating the windows with curtains pulled open. Nikki was there, staring out across the asphalt expanse toward the ocean. I watched as she changed out of pajamas, a strip tease with as much bravado as the dancers in the club. She saw me watching, blew me a kiss, and strolled into an adjoining bathroom, leaving the door ajar, leaving me to stare at the bare form behind frosted glass. I felt an urge to take her, or else to take her away.

11

SHADOW NATION

The lack of sleep was playing tricks on me. Early morning outside the strip club was surreal, stranger even than the events of the night before. The parking lot was a purgatory between the club and the outside world, an ecotone for cigarette butts, bottle shards, and weeds fighting to survive. For starters, Iman was tossing a tennis ball against the garage door. He was in a zone, not even bothering to look at the haggard adults blinking at the light. The film crew of regulars stood in a smoker's circle, with the usual conversation about how all of them had quit smoking. Irv was the culprit, holding a pack of Camel Lights in his shirt pocket like he was from a different era to lure them outside. I'd seen him pull this Pied Piper act quite a few times, and it made him leader of the pack. Literally. Alice had disappeared but Solomon emerged from the back seat of his gold Impala. He had a scratch on his right cheek and sauntered over in red Adidas sweats. He checked his phone as though it held the secret to the universe or at least to where the hell he'd disappeared to last night. The sun spritzed through a metallic haze of exhaust and smog, and the filtered light shone down on our strip club nation.

A white minivan with Utah plates from the last millennium wheeled down the alley. It inched along, at an impossibly slow speed, as though accustomed to navigating the world of drunken parishioners and kids flinging balls. The whole scene felt oddly familiar, like the soldiers between shifts killing time, a congregation of lost souls, and faces uneasy with sunlight. I was mystified by the colliding worlds. The minivan squeaked to a stop and two unlikely passengers revealed themselves: Nikki, opening the sliding doors, decked out in tight black leggings and a form-fitting blue tank top, and Alice at the wheel in a pink tracksuit and sunglasses with bulbous lenses that made her look like an insect. She gestured for us to enter like she was the queen bee to this hive-on-wheels. Obediently, everyone headed over to the rattling vehicle spewing fumes and climbed inside—except for Irv who took one last drag of his cigarette and tipped an imaginary cap to say goodbye.

Nikki moved to the back row to make room for the regulars, and, against my better judgment, I followed her. The seats filled up, with the front passenger seat left vacant for Iman.

On the dashboard was a collection of various frogs, everything from stuffed animals to plastic toys, including a frog bobblehead. Iman slid his ball and glove under his arm and petted the frogs, one at a time, with the tip of his index finger.

"Iman's the only one she lets touch them," Nikki whispered to me.

"That sounds filthy," I said in a low tone, our faces almost touching so that the other passengers couldn't listen in. "What the hell is going on here?"

"You mean you don't know?"

"I'm generally the last to know. That could be my tagline."

"It's cute. It makes me want to buy you."

I thought about continuing the banter, but her rich-girl comment stopped me in my tracks. Pops always said I wore my emotions on my sleeve, which made me a poor choice to pull into the various cons he pulled. She glanced over at me and read me like a book.

"Aw, did I hurt your feelings?" Nikki asked playfully.

The minivan made a long slow arc in the parking lot and rolled down the alley next to the Far Horizon warehouse. This was the same alley that ran toward the back garage to the Pourali residence.

"How come your mother lets you out to play with this crew?" I asked.

"She knows I need exercise," Nikki said. "She thinks it's good for me. And I have plenty of chaperones here."

"Exercise?"

"You know. Sweating. Fast heart rate. Panting." Nikki's hand slid across my leg and onto my crotch.

I placed my hand over hers to hide what she was doing and to keep myself from getting excited. This was every shade possible of wrong. I did nothing to move her hand as she massaged me through the thin cotton pants. I tried my best to to be quiet. Perhaps this was part of the family curse, to feel something approaching satisfaction before having it yanked out from under you.

The Far Horizon wasn't abandoned, far from it. Iman hung back with Nikki and me after we rolled through the back gate and parked next to a jet-black Mercedes. There were several luxury automobiles tucked away between the recycling dumpsters and the building. The kid let us know that the murdered-out luxury car with gold rims belonged to his Uncle Yar, just like the building itself. The warehouse was a repository for extra restaurant supplies for the Moroccan restaurant Baba, situated a few doors down from the strip club. It also provided office space for Yar, storage for an on-again-off-again import-export business, along with a few rooms that Solomon used for a recording studio as well as a small gym where he ran aerobics and spin classes to the strippers, belly dancers, and friends of both establishments. What the hell? Did the family own the entire block?

Alice led the way into the building with a key from her ring and disappeared up a back staircase while the rest of us shuffled over to the gym. A half-dozen women, including a dazed Tarzana and a few other dancers from the club, stretched out mats on the floor of a mammoth exercise room rigged with mirrors. The open space was in the center of the room, surrounded by exercise bikes, free weights, and treadmills. The bare beams and ducts of the rafters were the only thing that differentiated the space from a high-end private gym. There were several dancers from the club, one or two from the Goddess Guides party, and a few faces I didn't recognize. Maybe these women worked at

Yar's restaurant? Nikki joined the others in grabbing a mat and stretching.

Iman made a beeline past a ping pong table to the far side of the room and plunked himself down on a sofa to watch a soccer match already playing on a flat-screen TV. I felt lost until Solomon led me by my elbow between two exercise bikes and unlocked a door to an adjacent room. We slipped inside and he flicked on the lights to a small recording studio. Several guitars were perched on stands next to a full drum kit and bass. I recognized the scratched orange Gibson that Solomon had purchased from our summer jobs working as busboys—his first electric guitar. He led me to a desk covered in records and flipped through them like oversized baseball cards. Albums we grew up with flicked by and I thought about the hours we'd spent hanging out together, debating the worthiness of bands and tracks. Finally, he found what he was looking for—a hand mirror stashed in the stack. He pulled a small baggie of white crystals out of his front pocket and shook it.

"Lock the door, would you?" Solomon asked.

I shuffled back around to the entrance. Nikki winked at me from her mat before I shut and locked the door. By the time I turned around Solomon had already separated three lines and used the flat part of his driver's license to crush the meth, before flipping the card around and chopping it into lines. This was something I'd seen him do in New Orleans countless times, and I wasn't any stranger to occasional drug use. Truth was that I was tired, too, and in need of some conversation. This is one of the things about drug use that a lot of guys didn't want to admit. It was a way to get closer to your friends even as it took you farther from yourself.

Wordlessly, I accepted a rolled-up bill from Solomon's long outstretched fingers. I snorted a line and passed the money straw back to him. He quickly snorted up the other two and rubbed the bridge of his nose. It was almost like we were teenagers again, sneaking around behind our boss's back to get messed up. Only we weren't. We were adults. Or on the verge of something like it. The rush cleared away my cobwebs and made me alert to the oddity of the situation: our mutual employer, his extended family, the dynamics of the other shoe always feeling like it was about to drop.

"Damn, that's good shit," Solomon said.

"I'll take your word for it."

"You know that I know my drugs and my women."

"Which woman? Mona, who's sleeping with one brother Yar? Or Tarzana, who's sleeping with the other brother Big Z?"

"Damn, that's some smack talk. Buddy, the army has changed you."

"Not really. I still don't know a damn thing about women," I admitted. "Deirdre dumped me but definitely wanted to make it sting. I caught her fooling around with Miles, and she made sure I knew the trailer she bought with my money is in her name."

"Jesus," Solomon said. "She was always a bitch to people she didn't like. It's not personal. Would have happened sooner or later."

"I suppose. You always called her my drug. I should have listened to you."

"But you never do."

"You're one to talk." I shook my head at his offer for a line. "This shit can kill you if you do it long enough, but dealing it is just stupid."

"Like joining the army stupid or regular stupid?" He bobbed his head and more white powder disappeared.

"Don't change the subject. Not when you have gangbangers trying to mess you up. And why in the hell are you dealing drugs to a bunch of rich hippies?"

"Because it pays well and there's hot chicks willing to hang out with the guy who has a party in his pocket."

"This is dangerous."

"*Living* like we do is dangerous. I haven't changed. And neither have you. Dude, you think people need you to look out for them. Truth is, you need to look out for yourself."

"I can take care of myself."

"That's a matter of opinion. You can't help sticking your nose into things you shouldn't. Now Uncle Sam wants you. *Bad*. Do you really want to live off the grid?"

"I don't know what the hell I want."

"Jesus, your parents did a number on you. You still haven't gotten over that whole fucking mess."

"What mess?" I asked.

Solomon shrugged and opened his mouth several times like a fish tossed onto shore. "Don't do this. You know what mess. It's time for you to sort some things out for yourself."

Solomon slipped his license and baggie of crystals into his wallet. He rummaged inside a leather bag with a drawstring and pulled out a pair of black sweatpants with faded blue stripes. He stripped off his jeans and changed into workout clothes while I mulled over his words. What mess exactly did I need to sort out? My childhood was filled with loneliness and rebellion, parents focused on themselves, and an anger I could never really define. Solomon laced up his shoes before heading out into the exercise room with a booming, "Who wants to have a supreme ass?"

I was already a supreme ass, in my own way, so I decided to hightail it out of there. I holed up back in the minivan, in the back row, and stared at the warehouse. The Far Horizon's logo shimmered in the blossoming day, the fuzziness of the world around me and my vampiric brethren from the club, like the daydream that is life.

I have always been susceptible to these fading moments, alone, staring into space. The details were beyond me, the flotsam of the river from my childhood and other rivers, all my memories hovering like some movie I'd watched while sleeping and could almost recall. I felt the world pour into the seat beside me, felt Nikki slipping out early from the workout, her sticky body next to mine, taking my manhood into her mouth.

The horizon danced with silhouettes, a motorcycle and a

man; it was Mitzu dismounting, placing riding gloves into his helmet and trudging toward the back entrance of the warehouse. His head swiveled, independently of his body, or so it seemed. His eyes met mine and he grinned at me as though I were a sandwich, then a friend. He disappeared or was he never really there? I thought I saw him framed beside Malik, one per window on the second floor, two eyes of a mystery that was overwhelming me. In the periphery, I sensed a body sinking into the ground, a feeling I've had my entire life, danger stalking me in every port, every place. My breath heaved and my voice rattled in low moans as I came for the first time in months.

What was real anymore? I woke up, startled by the motion of the vehicle and swallowing a shriek, the sun burning through the window in the back of the minivan. Alice parked the rattling behemoth in the back of Solomon's apartment complex. She took up two spots and I tried to play off my surprise at our arrival. Had I been snoring? What the hell did Malik think about their bouncer and family protection snoozing on duty? Hell, was I even ever off duty? I wondered if anyone had seen Nikki sneak outside or whether I should trust my memories.

The outside door to the minivan swung open. I tried to play off the nap and quietly followed Solomon and Tarzana up the back steps. My legs were stiff and my crotch was sticky. Alice locked up her vehicle with a frog key chain. She trailed behind me with a distant smile that seemed pointed at a hole in the ozone above us. I was bone-tired, as though I'd just finished a double shift on guard duty back in Kabul. I paused at the top of the stairwell and stared back at Alice. She nodded as though reading my mind and said, "A lot of the dancers live here. Malik owns the place, of course."

"Of course, their family seems to own just about everything," I muttered.

"Don't forget everyone," Alice added.

"Yes, how could I forget that?"

She held on to my wrist like a child and pulled me to her

while Solomon and Tarzana made their way into his apartment. The movement was more protective than sexual, but I don't think that's what Solomon thought. My oldest friend shot me a knowing look before disappearing inside. Who could blame him for leaving me behind in a lifetime of me chasing after him? I already knew what was going to happen next. There would be a noisy coupling with the bedroom door slightly ajar, the couch I now called home too close to the action to drown out the racket even with the help of the computer speakers.

"You're with me," Alice said.

"I'm not that kind of boy," I protested halfheartedly.

"You definitely are," she said. "But it won't matter. You'll see."

Alice led me inside the apartment next door to Solomon's and directed me to an immaculate olive-green couch as though it were being displayed in a showroom. She propped a pillow under my head, flipped off my shoes, and stretched me out. The light flickered through thin curtains and washed over an apartment that was as carefully kept as Solomon's was cluttered. The only objects not purely functional were a mishmash of frogs on the mantel surrounding a framed photo of a five-year-old boy. I thought about asking Alice about the kid, but she was already in motion, turning on the television to an episode of *I Love Lucy*. Alice smiled at me sadly as though even laughter from the past was etched with pain.

I cupped my head around my face, trying not to give away how tired I was, how much I missed having someone or something to hold on to. Solomon was a train wreck, but he was right about me. I'd always kept my eyes on those around me rather than look out for myself. It made me a spectator in a world that catered to the bold. It drove me to the fringes. Alice sat beside me and there was something primal in the way she stroked my hair. I wondered if she was the mother of the boy on the mantel. Sleep carried me away, before I could ask her about her past. The worry was still there, but I was gone.

I'm not sure how long I'd spaced out. Somewhere along the way the shrill laughter of Lucille Ball had flipped to the wry sarcasm of Elizabeth Montgomery in *Bewitched*, the pretext of witchery always present for women, just as men are helpless in the face of everyday magic. Alice was no longer next to me. Her bedroom door was cracked open and a shadow fluttered past. The haze in the LA sky and lack of a watch made me wonder if she was preparing for bed or already getting up for her next shift at Club Paradise.

Alice's living room felt even emptier without her. I wandered to the bathroom and flicked on the faucet. Water streamed into my cupped hands, and I splashed my face. Here I was in the desert, with my skin parched, and the hot curse of the swamps was hunting me. I could feel the steam of it behind me and in front of me. I looked away from a two-day stubble in the mirror that made me look older than I had any right, my mother's brown eyes and broad nose projecting like a swollen grape, but my father's coloring and face from the cheeks downward. The bathroom did not have more than the bare essentials: no towels or dirty clothes hanging on hooks, no grime or stains on tile, no trash in the can or hair dryer on the countertop. It was as though Alice were floating through life, half-ghost, visitor even in her home.

The bathroom window was cracked open and there was a fist-sized gap between two sunflowers in her lace curtains. I peered out onto the stairwell outside Solomon's apartment. On his front stoop, a hooded figure collected a plastic Gap bag from my best friend. I doubted this was an exchange of jeans, though. Solomon stepped back and the door shut. The man spun around before darting down the steps. It was Ricki Ticki, the asshole drug dealer I'd locked horns with. Apparently, he no longer wanted to hurt Solomon. Allegiances had shifted. The shadows of the handrails tattooed the wood in a jagged line toward Alice's front door. It was beautiful and it would not last. Nothing was what it appeared to be.

12

Shadow Boss

One day you're here…and the next? Tarzana's disappearance wasn't so strange in a revolving door of life off the grid. Club Paradise and its clientele thrived on anonymity. The women were constantly coming and going. The dance of fake names and tall tales at the strip club reminded me of the shadows of myself. We each had our uniform and role to play at Club Paradise, not unlike my old army platoon where the prisoners donned blue overalls, the guards sported camouflage, and occasional visitors strutted around in civies, each form of dress carrying a different status.

I wondered what the OGA (an acronym for Other Government Agencies like the CIA) had felt like strolling through Bagram Air Base, dressed as though they were camping or in a back-slapping beer commercial, with the power to pop open men like piñatas or stash them away like popsicles in GTMO. Being a prison guard had given me endless time to let my imagination run wild as I accompanied the prisoners to and from their interrogations. I was never trusted to watch the OGA practice their trade, however. That honor went to Staff Sergeant Lasicky. He gladly stayed for these marathon sessions. All I ever saw was the wreckage of the men afterward, the worry lines on their skin reminiscent of the faded Cyrillic on the walls of the airbase from Russian soldiers who behind unheeded warnings.

The helplessness I felt in that haunted place in the mountains filled me with so much rage that I released it in one punch. I'd left Lasicky bloodied on the airstrip at Barksdale just minutes after landing back home in Louisiana and that was the end of the man formerly known as Buddy Rivet. All I'd done was punished myself for the terror, real and imagined, going on behind closed doors. I was now pinned against the ocean with my fake name while Lasicky was probably getting pinned with another medal even as the war in Afghanistan ended. For the time being. It's strange how those in power and those without power intersect in a world of false intentions. In that way the military and the strip club were alike. I'd never discovered Tarzana's real name, just as she'd never know mine. She told us at the bar one night that she chose her stripper name because she grew up in Tarzana and because her dead father had loved Tarzan films. When the erotic dancer vanished without a trace, who did I imagine would be looking for her? Hell, who was looking for me? Tarzana simply disappeared one night before her shift. Poof. It was as though she'd tumbled through the slats in Solomon's futon into some other dimension like the kids in *The Lion, the Witch and the Wardrobe*. Women revolved quickly through the club and through Solomon's bedroom, as if there was a trap door.

Tarzana was replaced quickly enough on stage and at a Solomon's pad by a dancer who wore seven different outfits matching the color of the rainbow. She quickly became a part of the club's mystique, and it was because of her that *Blue-Beer Mondays* and *Red-Light Thursdays* were coined, with gimmicky specials at the bar. Solomon's new girlfriend of the moment was chatty and cast a web of stories of fallen Hollywood icons she'd known and demanded that we call her by the color of the day. I called her Crayola behind her back and I saw my pal get to sleep with all of the hues of the rainbow. The mystery novels I read to pass the time were color-themed too. I powered through Travis McGee books at the rate of one per week: *Nightmare in Pink, Pale Gray for Guilt, A Purple Place for Dying*.

I hadn't spoken to Solomon much recently, but this was as much a byproduct of me hanging out at Alice's as it was from the rift that had opened between us. Also, there was nothing about my nature that made it easy for me to sit by while my oldest friend put himself in danger. He was either dealing drugs or enabling it at the club. I was a lot of things, but casual wasn't one of them. This was also one of the reasons why I couldn't stop thinking about Nikki. Her plea for help had stuck with me, along with her flirting, and I found myself thinking about her on the other side of the walls of Club Paradise. Her mother ruled that kingdom and I couldn't help but wonder what role she played on this side of the wall.

One night after a particularly draining shift I decided to crash on Alice's couch even though her sometimes boyfriend, Blake, the ex-NSA bar regular, tagged along. Solomon was out on a solo gig as DJ with the Goddess Guides—he'd stopped asking me to go along with him. He could sense my disapproval of his extra-curricular activities, and I needed to get a few hours of uninterrupted sleep before the after-afterparty returned to his pad. Besides, Flynn had already pulled me aside and told me that I needed to be back at the club at nine a.m. sharp to chauffeur Iman to some appointment.

I opened a window and kept an eye on the walkway outside Solomon's apartment while I read the odd assortment of science magazines in Alice's apartment. I read about the possibilities of organic computing and how machines modeled on the mind would be able to process information in ways that would change the world. Not sure a machine based on my mind would be worth a damn. I sensed shadows flitting across the porch but nothing was there when I looked. The hours passed and I never saw Solomon return. I never remembered falling asleep.

In the morning, I joined Alice in reading the LA Times, while Blake cooked breakfast. We soon got into a spirited discussion about the Pouralis. It felt relatively normal—the smell of pancakes on the stove, something I'd missed in my time in Afghanistan—as we joked about the dual lives of Big Z and his family. Blake was several inches shorter than Alice, with short-cropped curly hair and a permanent five o'clock shadow. He wore one of her short robes with a casual disregard that we might see his junk while pacing around the kitchen like an aged Tigger.

"Big Z likes calling the shots in the club, but I have a feeling he's a pushover at home," Blake said.

"Aren't all guys this way?" I asked, well into my second pancake, impatiently using the prongs of the forks to tear off strips instead of cutting with a knife. I knew my table etiquette had suffered from too much time in the mess hall.

"Nikki is the one that scares me the most," Alice teased. "And not just because she's making goo-goo eyes at West."

"What makes you think that?"

"I have my sources," Alice said. "You better make sure Big Z doesn't catch wind of it."

"I think Bianca might be the really scary one," I said, trying to change the subject.

"Big Z keeps the wife and daughter locked inside what's effectively a prison, and you two fear the women?" Blake asked.

"They control things behind the scenes. Believe me. You should know," Alice said.

"Listening in on someone is very different from controlling them."

"Information is power," I said.

"Money is even more power," Blake said, sliding a couple pieces of bacon onto my plate. "All of the cash in Club Paradise funnels up to Big Z or Malik. Even the rental of the basement to film our movie is split between the two of them."

"There's a lot you don't know," Alice said, looking almost matronly in a pair of black sweats that dominated her wardrobe in between dancing.

"You don't think I have my ear to the ground in that place?" Blake asked. "I pay for the privilege of hanging out in a den of vipers. That doesn't mean I don't know how dangerous it is for the hired help."

Blake winked at me and raised his bushy eyebrows. He beamed at Alice, but she'd already turned her head toward the photo of the boy on the mantel. There was a moment of almost silence, with the thrum of freeway traffic rolling through the shaded windows. The cooking utensils that Blake had used were drying in the dish drainer—condensation gathered on the tip of the spatula and I waited for the drop to fall, for some clue to emerge in the silence.

"You're a voyeur, not a spy. That's why you sabotaged yourself," Alice said. "Some of us watch. Others hurt other people. Some of us do both."

"Don't forget that I write poetry. That might have had something to do with it," Blake said.

"A poet who doesn't write is like a mother with no kids," Alice rose and wandered into her bedroom, pancake half-eaten, and shut the door.

"Poetry?" I asked.

"It's a long story. My father's an English professor. He named me after the poet William Blake."

"He's cool. We read a few of his poems in high school."

"When I was working for the NSA, I hated my boss and played a practical joke on him. I forwarded emails from some crackpot. Because of my father, I knew that the messages contained William Blake's poetry, all garbled together. Just damn poetry. The NSA spent a lot of time and money tracking the dude posting this work online, looking for hidden messages."

"How did they know you knew it was Blake?"

"I trusted the wrong person with my joke. It got me kicked out of the agency."

"Did your boss get in trouble?" I asked.

"God, I hope so. He was a dick. Probably not, though."

Our stories weren't all that different. Blake had his own Lasicky. He also had a brother looking out for him by giving him a gig at his company just like Solomon had given me a chance to reboot my life by working at the club. Maybe the real friction came from the fact that Solomon was as disappointed in me as I was in him.

"Don't you ever worry the NSA is tracking you?"

"All the time," Blake said. "They can listen in to anything they want from any computer, any phone, any video game console. I just hope to stay under the radar."

"You and me both," I said.

"The government isn't who you have to worry about."

"Not sure I follow," I said. Blake was part paranoid and part bullshitter, but still might be telling the truth.

"How do you think I came to start hanging out at Club Paradise?"

"Alice?"

"No, dude, she's why I stay. That clan mother Bianca hired me freelance to wire the whole place for sound. Everywhere."

"How much can she hear?" I asked.

"Every fucking thing," Blake whispered, and cleared his throat. "Keep yourself together when you're there."

"Thanks for the breakfast and the advice." I stuffed half a pancake into my mouth and handed him the plate before heading for the door. Looks like I may have been right about Bianca after all.

There was a lot for me to learn about Los Angeles. I rarely ventured outside of the neighborhood surrounding the strip club. My borders were Venice Beach and UCLA, Century City and a neighborhood off Wilshire called Tehrangeles. In a short drive you could get to a whole lot of places, including the border of Beverly Hills. That was where I found myself that morning, chauffeuring Iman to a private country club called Oakwood. Something wasn't right, though, with the kid.

When I'd arrived at the back of Club Paradise, Flynn flung me the keys to the town car, eager to get some shuteye himself. Iman was already sitting in the back of the running vehicle. He was usually a chatterbox with tons of attitude, but I couldn't get two words out of him on the commute. Iman was dressed in white shorts and a white polo shirt with his nose in a tablet the whole drive over to Oakwood. Probably some video game or music video. Hell, could be porn for all I knew. I'd never seen the kid with either parent, and he had the same smart-ass attitude of the latchkey kids from my own childhood. I followed the route that Flynn had set into the GPS and pulled up to a guard station, manned by two guys falling into middle age with deep creases in their foreheads, both bald, joking in some Eastern European language. They glanced at my face and began a conversation that rattled on for nearly a minute.

Jesus, did they need me to cough up my ID? I'd already trashed my real driver's license and I wasn't anxious to test the fake one that Solomon had helped me score. I fumbled in my pockets and tried to come up with some bullshit story.

Thankfully, Iman shouted from the back: "Let us through, fuckheads!"

Either the guards recognized the car or Iman or both and waved us ahead. I saluted like a civilian, with two fingers on the brim of an invisible hat and rolled around to visitor parking.

"Remind me not to get on your bad side," I muttered to see if I could cheer up the kid.

"You're reminded. But I'm not the Pourali you need to worry about."

Again, the warnings. How bad was this family, really? The kid was likely messing with my head, but I couldn't help myself from thinking about each of the Pouralis, and the various dangers they posed.

Everything at the Oakwood Country Club was a shade of white: buildings, pool umbrellas, pressed staff uniforms, sand hazards on the golf course, even the umbrellas in the drinks. A weathered black concierge, playing the role of doorman, opened the frosted glass door. I couldn't help but notice that the hired help in this place showed the diversity of Los Angeles. Did Iman feel out of his comfort zone here too? I played the roll of servant, all smiles and nods, toting the kid's tennis gear in a gym bag with an emblazoned Oakwood logo. I trailed several steps behind as Iman hauled ass through the mammoth facility. We jetted past a sauna and masseuse tables, a coffee cart and business center, and back outside where a path forked toward either a driving range or tennis courts.

I struggled not to fall behind and thought about teasing

the kid about his preppie outfit but thought better of it. He was all elbows and knees marching to the tennis courts, barely even nodding to the buff male tennis pro before beginning his instruction. I'm not sure whether Iman was embarrassed or just pissed off, but he didn't shoot me a glance as I circled behind him. The courts, a dozen in all, were well maintained. They were filled with retirees and trust-funders of both sexes volleying in the late morning LA haze. Dressed in black pants and T-shirt, I was invisible in this place of leisure, the hired help. Babysitter. Bodyguard. Bored. The fences were covered in a felt the color of money to keep out the sunlight.

My time at the court, as with all things, was non-committal. My back rested against the fence post, with one leg resting on the asphalt court, the other on the manicured grass between the court and outdoor café. Purgatory was my natural state, resting between worlds. I closed my eyes and breathed in the scent of roasted chicken wafting from the nearby kitchen and let the whacking of tennis balls draw me into a type of mediation. I had let this whole notion of a family curse get to me far too much. I was very like an animal frozen on the yellow line of a freeway, traffic whizzing by on either side. I was afraid to move, to commit to anything or anyone, the possibility of roadkill more likely by the moment.

There was a rustling beside me, and I caught a whiff of perfume that was almost edible. The hairs on my neck stood on end and I reacted without thinking. I spun from one fence post to the other, startling a woman with red hair, model height, impressive calves in too-small shorts and a T-shirt. Green eyes flashed as she fumbled a cell phone into the grass. "Shit," she said. "You're like a nervous cat. Don't just stand there. Pick the goddamn thing up."

The voice wasn't familiar, but the cadence and tone were clearly that of Iman's mother. "Please let me get that for you, Bianca," I said, leaning down, gripping the phone, and holding it out as a peace offering.

"Don't bother. It's yours." Her mouth curled so that I could catch a glimpse of looks that must have caused car accidents back in the day.

"I don't know if it's a good idea for me to be accepting gifts from my employer," I said.

"God, you're dense. It's not a gift. It's your new work phone."

"No thanks."

"Yes thanks," she said. "It's not an option. I need you to be more available."

"I already work when and where you say."

"Good. I just need you to be more flexible. Your primary job is no longer security at Club Paradise. I'm going to need you to focus on taking my family places, running errands, providing extra muscle at times, and watching my husband."

"Your husband? Don't I work for—"

"Me? Yes. And don't interrupt. You're my employee. You'll do what I ask when I ask. No questions asked."

"Isn't that a lot to ask?"

"I don't think so, Buddy."

I thought about walking away right then and there. Lord knows if I'd had any sense, I would've headed for the nearest army base and thrown myself at the mercy of the government. I was snared already in the web of this family, though. I found myself wanting to protect Nikki and Iman from their father and his business dealings. Also, there was something about this woman I recognized. She was accustomed to using men like props, the way the interrogators used ordinary things, like a boom box, to do horrible things to prisoners. She was fighting tooth and nail for something she believed in—her family. Besides, Solomon, Alice, and the others at the club were at the mercy of Big Z and Malik, and someone needed to be there to keep the peace. Bianca's offer wasn't much, but it was all I had.

"Whatever it is you think you have on me, you don't," I said.

"And still, you'll make me proud. I know you will." She paused at the end of her sentence, a mocking note filled with a hint of disdain. "Keep the goddamn phone charged, and make sure you check it. Often. I'll have things for you to do."

Iman, impatient with a series of forehands, placed two hands on his racket. He launched a ball, with his backhand, over the green partition and onto the roof of the café.

"Like watching your son wish he was playing baseball?"

"Oh, yes," Bianca said, leaning in close. She brushed her breasts against my arm and shoved the prong end of the cell-phone charger into my palm. "You'll watch a lot of people suffer. You won't be able to help yourself."

I was speechless as she stormed away. Part of me couldn't help looking at her ass, even though there wasn't anything about this woman I remotely liked. I turned to catch Iman staring at me, a look on his face that was somewhere between incredulity and anger, either for me witnessing his emasculation or else wondering how his mother could be at the same club and not even stop by to say *hello*.

13

DRUNKEN SHADOWS

What the hell was going on? I was trying damn hard to get off the grid and thought I'd scored a perfect gig. That is until some woman managed to find out who I was and placed me in harm's way by turning me into her errand boy. There was a huge difference between hanging out in a strip club and zipping around town in daylight, putting myself in danger of being spotted or breaking the law. Jaywalking could get me into Fort Leavenworth. Trying to stay undercover after going AWOL was now as complicated, seemingly, as my relationship with the Pouralis.

After Iman's tennis lesson I looped around the club, waiting for the kid to be done with his shower. I avoided the signs leading to the golf course and found myself pacing poolside in a circuit around the gym. I was stressed out and it automatically made me feel better to walk. I felt paranoid, even though there was no reason to be. I imagined that dude with a crew cut, sitting in a lounge chair was an army officer on leave. I worried that someone on staff would ask me for ID and detain me until the police came. I imagined myself in a cell and it made me speed up my pace even more. On my third lap around the pool, a wet towel landed on my shoulder.

I spun to see Nikki, in a flimsy two-piece white bikini, catching rays on a beach chair next to a brunette her own age with a perky nose, perma-smile, and curves. She grinned at me and snapped her fingers.

"West, would you be a dear and get me a fresh towel?" she asked, her voice slurred. It looked like Nikki had managed to sneak a few drinks at the club.

"Sure thing," I said, trying hard to look nonchalant, worried that her parents or brother Malik were nearby.

I hurried over to the kiosk where the towels were dispensed and dropped the old one into the used hamper. Instead of asking the woman on duty for a towel, I waited until she was helping another club member with sunscreen. I reached over her cart and snatched two new towels. I didn't want to chance that Nikki's friend wanted one too. Both women were giggling by the time I returned. I set the towels on the glass table between them.

"Is it true that Nikki can give you any order whatsoever and you have to follow it?" the brunette asked.

"I don't normally share personal info with someone I don't know," I said.

"West, this is Betsy. Betsy, this is my sexy manservant."

"Hi, Betsy, I work for Nikki's parents. My job is to protect her—"

"From boredom," Nikki joked. I'd meant to say from *bad influences like you*, but Nikki had beaten me to the punch. "Betsy, isn't he a tall glass of water?"

"I'd go lesbo for a threesome with you guys," Betsy said, loud enough to wake the man with the crew cut, who looked like he wanted to strangle all of us.

I kept swiveling to make sure a Pourali wasn't sneaking up on me and to see if Iman had emerged. And I sure as hell didn't want to draw the attention of the country club staff.

"What's up, West? Do you have to pee?" Nikki asked, continuing her apparent quest to embarrass me as much as possible.

"Just strip and piss in the pool. Lord knows that's what we do," Betsy said.

The man with the crew cut shook his head angrily and launched himself over to the kiosk. I didn't want to wait around to see what happened next. I muttered, "See you later," and hurried toward the gym entrance. For once, luck was with me. Iman emerged, his wet hair slicked back like his older brother's. We moved in unison like soldiers as we wordlessly marched to the country club parking lot, the laughter of two women following us on our journey out.

My life at Club Paradise as I'd formerly known it was over. Just minutes after I dropped Iman and the town car off at the garage, I got a text from Bianca to *hang out with the regulars*. Looked like from then on, I'd be getting my marching orders from a phone. The sun was difficult to place in the overcast sky. It was just after two p.m., but it could have been later or earlier. The haze had been impenetrable for a week, unlike the sun, moon, and stars that felt so low in Kabul that you imagined you could pluck them from the sky as easily as you could lemons from one of the trees at my new apartment complex.

A strange sight met me at the door—it was Mitzu dressed in black pants and T-shirt, but he wasn't there with Yar. He scrunched his face like he'd just swallowed a too-spicy pepper and I could sense the anger simmering in his clenched muscles. I refused to make eye contact until I could figure out what was going on. I slid past him into the main bar and couldn't help noticing a tattoo on his bicep of a court jester brandishing a set of claws. What the hell was that supposed to mean?

All the regulars were already there. Before I could start my babysitting shift, Flynn ducked out from behind the bar and pulled me into the vacant DJ booth. Looking around like someone was watching, he told me that Mitzu had taken over my shifts. Apparently, the Pouralis were used to sharing their employees between family members and businesses. During our chat all I could think about was what Blake had told me about the place being bugged.

"Be careful," Flynn whispered to me before heading back to his station. "You took Mitzu's place in the organization."

Organization? What kind of language was that? I circled around a few lackadaisical dancers and settled into a seat next to Judd at the bar. Today, I didn't have any paperback to distract me, so I found myself discussing everything from the legalization of marijuana to the drunkest celebrity to have ever rolled into the club. There was a strange energy in the air, and I sensed the gang had a collective mission to get wasted. Judd, normally with his nose stuck in his artist's notebook, was already hammered and unusually talkative. He'd found a blender and was churning out shakes for lunch, with a combination of vodka and rum. Deacon, during one of our long night shifts, had told me the story of how Judd's father had started the company *Lifelong,* a multi-billion-dollar multilevel marketing company that sold protein shakes, vitamins, and personal care products across the globe and always seemed to be in the news for the wrong reason. "The kid comes here to piss off the old man," Deacon had told me. I wondered what Judd's old man would think about him fixing up Orange Blastberries, Mochachillaxers, and Mintilla Gorillas for the crew. Apparently, these shakes were chock full of protein, and gave you the craps if you didn't mix in some roughage. Judd didn't pull any punches when complaining about his father's company or the products they hawked to the masses.

I found myself getting drunk, something I swore I wouldn't do on the job. It was stupid, misplaced rage for feeling out of control and trapped in a web of emotions I didn't understand. On my new phone, I placed another message on the Lake Charles Craig's List board, this time posting Pops' name backward and my phone number. I wasn't even sure what I'd say if he contacted me. Moms was a lost cause, but there was something in my past flittering around the shadows that I couldn't see, couldn't understand. It scared me.

Later that afternoon a familiar-looking man strolled into the bar but didn't want anything to do with the dancers. He was all business and walked a bit like a human Slinky, all springs and coils. I found out later that the guy had been Flynn's roommate and was a character actor in a wide range of films. Even someone like me who never recognized anyone on the covers of magazines got a case of déjà vu. Flynn huddled with his old roomie at the far end of the bar. Whatever they were discussing was intense. Everyone here had a secret life, some other existence outside of the club that got absorbed into the collective unease inside these walls. Alice had been surly ever since she

came on shift and waved off Blake's offer to buy her a drink. I
thought about going over to cheer her up, but she was deep in
conversation on her phone.

"She wasting money on a damn psychic," Blake muttered
across the bar. "She spends half her tips on some charlatan
named Zelda." I found myself thinking about the Azores psychic who warned me: *You will face decisions that could hurt you or
people you love.* She'd been right about the curse, about the dead
zone surrounding me. Perhaps some people had the ability to
see past the murk surrounding sinners like us.

Alice sat in her usual booth but wasn't the magnet she normally was for the other dancers in distress. She was stressed out
in a way I'd never seen. She poured herself into her call like it
was a pool without a bottom. From my perch next to the kitch-
en window, I had a panoramic view of the staff and customers.
All of us here were complicit in creating or keeping secrets,
whether it was the shame of stripping or a significant other at
home wondering how money disappeared from the bank ac-
count, or those on the fringe, like myself, looking to hide. The
victims were endless: the women selling themselves for tips and
the customers that the Pouralis drained of cash were two sides
of the same coin. For some reason, Salt and Spokane seemed
the loneliest of all. They'd built their relationship in a place of
darkness and obsession, filmmakers caught in a bizarre fairy-
tale world with no one to free them.

The lack of lighting in the bar was there to keep everyone
from looking too hard at anything or anyone. I felt a panic,
not unlike the fear of stepping on a bomb. The Pourali family
seemed eager to join me in the unraveling of their own heritage
and past. I wasn't sure whether Big Z had fled Iran with his
parents when it became ultra-religious. The wrestler's accent
showed a family in transition, and the desire, apparently, to shed
past traditions even while attempting to keep his family safe.
The window shutters in the club whirred closed as day fell to
night, and I felt as if I'd lost several hours.

"Judd, these shakes have given me the shakes. I need real

food," Irv complained. "And my stomach can't handle another grease-bomb taco from the kitchen."

"Spokane could use a real meal for once," Salt said, running her fingers into the crook of her partner's elbow. Spokane had a stone-faced expression that could have meant anything—that he wanted to kill her, or he wanted to rumba on the roof, or that he was sleepy. I'd never heard the director say more than a few words.

"How about a road trip?" Blake asked, his voice slurred from a day of drinking.

"Hell yeah!" Judd said, his energy propelling him and the barflies into a standing position.

In my pocket, the phone buzzed and there was a text from Bianca: *Take them down the block to Baba.*

"Hey, guys," I said. "I know the perfect place and it's just a few doors down." The regulars turned to look at me in surprise, and I waved them toward the door.

Maybe I was ready to get clear of the bar for a while. Maybe I was sick of the fried bar food. Maybe I was looking to make a good impression on Bianca so that she would let me drive Nikki to some future destination. Maybe I was the Pied Piper of the damned. I led the drunken posse past the main stage, the red velvet curtains, and Mitzu's stare and out into the gray night.

The interior of Baba was filled with Asian tourists and after-work hipsters from neighboring businesses. It smelled of Middle Eastern food and. the decor reminded me of Club Paradise, a cheap Hollywood set mimicking the inside of a sultan's palace. It was as though the architect had moved down the block from the castle and moved down in budget. The menu, posted on the front arch, was printed on a washed yellow parchment with cursive script. It detailed a mishmash of cuisines from various Mediterranean countries. The lighting was dim and the place was just starting to get hopping. We heard the jangling of a belly dancer in another room and horn-laded music from ceiling speakers. A hostess, with black eye makeup and fingernails, led us to a private alcove in the back of the restaurant. It It must have been because we were a big party, or they wanted to cordon us off because we were wasted. I trailed uncomfortably behind the regulars, not sure how this strange babysitting was supposed to work.

At a table in the corner next to the kitchen entrance, Yar was having dinner with Malik. Of course, Big Z's cousin must be the owner. They were both rifling through an open manila folder with papers fanning out between cocktails. Neither of them had noticed our arrival and I didn't wait around in the doorway. The last thing I wanted was for either of them to see me drunk.

We sat on floor cushions around a rectangular table lit barely enough for us to see our menus. Not that it mattered. Irv was well ahead of us. He excelled at ordering for the group at Club Paradise: food, drinks, lap dances. He quickly settled on the sampler platter along with several bottles of wine, and they made me track down a waitress to put in the order. One of the bottles was finished before the appetizers came. I was thankful that I was wedged in next to Spokane, as I wasn't particularly in a talkative mood. Why exactly was it so important that I babysit this crew tonight? It could be pure economics. The regulars spent a fortune every night at the club. Was I there to protect their investment and make sure their money stayed inside the family businesses?

I looked around the table at the strange crew. Irv was progressively growing more gray hair below his forehead as his own dome thinned. He was red-faced from drinking, but talkative, used to giving his opinion on all matters. Irv thrived on being the financier and producer for the B horror films they shot in the basement, always on the brink of a distribution deal in Asia or Canada, a man out of touch and out of time. Judd, the artist, wore flannel pants and a jean shirt, a guy who liked bucking fashion trends. His face, as usual, was in his notebook. He traced the pattern from the walls as a tattoo on the arm of a self-portrait. He was only here because he didn't like living in the shadow of a CEO father labeled as a pyramid schemer. Blake seemed to have family money, but he was the only one who worked anywhere near normal hours. I could tell that his feelings for Alice were part of why he hung out, his NSA stalking inclinations focused squarely on his somewhat girlfriend. Salt didn't hide her age; she proudly wore silver streaks in her hair that made it even clearer that she was Spokane's patron. Half of her conversations were about how talented a photographer and director Spokane was. He wore sports coats and only talked about baseball, women, and weather, like he was from some past era. He never ever seemed to get drunk even though he spent all his time trying.

Halfway through dinner, a belly dancer flitted into the alcove for a session with us, having made her way across the restaurant. What the hell? It was Tarzana, now a blond instead of a brunette, with a single dark lock, her eyes unfocused, and her movements disjointed. She was doped up, that much was clear. For starters, she didn't track who we were. She'd given a lap dance to everyone in the room before. Except me...I didn't cross that line. She reminded me of a butterfly trapped indoors, shimmying from place to place, her belly undulating, the folds of her stomach mesmerizing.

"You like her, don't you?" Salt whispered into Spokane's ear. "She's hot. Enjoy yourself."

Salt excused herself. Irv, Blake, and Judd watched Tarzana intently. Spokane just stared at his empty glass and muttered under his breath, loud enough for me to hear, "Salt left so I could enjoy myself. She's thoughtful that way."

"Lucky guy," was all I could think to say, even though I didn't believe my own words.

His eyes darted to the side and locked on mine. "God, I hate her. I hate 'em all."

By the time I needed to make a trip to the bathroom, Malik and Yar were no longer seated at the side table. I was having a hard time figuring out what they'd been meeting about. Did it have anything to do with Goddess Guides or the drug dealer I'd seen popping by the first time I visited Alice's place? The inside of the men's room had a framed poster depicting Barbara Eden in *I Love Jeannie*. Of course, someone had etched a penis in the Plexiglas near her mouth—from a set of car keys most likely.

The bathroom was empty and the music from the restaurant sifted through as if it came from another world. As I was washing my hands and looking at myself in the cracked mirror, a figure darted past. It was a girl barely old enough to run, three years old or so, disappearing into the only stall, the door swinging closed behind her. I turned off the tap and nudged the door open, revealing a stained toilet but no girl, no one in the bathroom with me. It was as if she'd disappeared into the toilet, descending into the pipes beneath the city, into the sludge that ran its course to the ocean...to nothingness. Sleep deprivation made me dreamier than usual, or I was losing it.

My phone buzzed and I wondered if Bianca knew I was derelict in my duties. The message was from an unknown number: *Cheer up, kiddo*. It must be Pops, reminding me to keep things light, not that it had ever worked. Not that I wasn't a walking basket case.

Outside the bathroom, I almost ran straight into Tarzana dabbing at her eyes with a balled-up tissue. "West, what the fuck am I doing here?" she sobbed.

"I could ask myself the same question," I said, not knowing what to do. My conversations with Tarzana had been about growing up in the valley. She'd shared stories of her "ho" friends who wanted to be movie stars and the drug-addled hours she'd spent pretending she was living in TV shows like *Buffy the Vampire Slayer*.

"I'm like an animal to them. First, they use you to do things and then they eat you alive."

Tarzana's pupils were dilated, two moons of terror. "Is there a friend you can go to? Your parents? I'm not sure I know how to help you."

She laughed but it sounded like someone getting punched in

the solar plexus. "As soon as that dickhead Big Z screwed me, I started getting the bad shifts at Paradise. Big Z, what a joke. They should call him Little Z."

"Why are you working here?"

"After I complained, Big Z screwed me again. He told me the only job available was to work for his cousin Yar, who's an even worse pig."

"Why don't you leave?" I asked

"Why don't *you* leave?"

"Maybe because I haven't been screwed enough yet," I said, and a helpless feeling filled my head, a shadowy land behind my eyes that would never burn off.

"First, they hook you on drugs and then they make you do more and more degrading things." Her voice hardened. "Then you like doing those things."

"Hey, there are always options."

"For some people."

"I'll walk you to a motel. You can get a good night's sleep and figure out what's next."

"Another man is already paying for that right," she said. "I'm damaged goods."

"You're a person, not a thing."

She stared at the floor where a corner of a Persian rug curled up next to the door of the women's bathroom. She smoothed it with her foot and glanced over her shoulder before stumbling into the john. "Do yourself a favor, West, and get as far away from the Pouralis as you can."

The door creaked shut. The exit sign at the end of the hall-way flickered in syncopation with the music. That was the last time I ever saw her.

14

SHADOW ROMANCE

Some say that your mother is your first love. If so, I was unlovable. Moms had a way of looking out for herself. Pops thought she couldn't help herself. Moms gravitated to the spotlight and lived for applause. She sang duets with Solomon's mom on the *Aces*, always stealing the limelight, prancing into the audience to sit on the laps of men. Pops called them marks. In between dealing cards, he would overhear Moms in conversation, and later they would hatch their cons. This is what hurt me most of all, I think. These anonymous men hanging on her arm, looking to bed her, always getting her attention, her smile, her love in short doses. It was more than I ever got, and I ended up hating her for bringing me into the world and then making it clear that I was in her way. It could've been the alcohol making me feel sorry for myself.

After staying up all night, I was finally sober. I'd followed the stumbling regulars to the basement and watched Alice try to navigate the drunken crew in a scene that took multiple takes and trips upstairs for coffee. I ended up at the top of the tower at sunrise to see if I could signal Nikki. I'd been thinking about her all night. Alice and Solomon had tried, in their own ways, to convince me to stay clear of her, but I wondered if Nikki and I had something in common—a desire to free ourselves from our pasts.

When the sunlight triggered the electronic shades to open, I looked into Nikki's room. There was no sign of her in there. Her bed was empty, and her bathroom door was closed. The tower smelled faintly of turpentine and perfume. I wondered what scurried in the corners and if the monthly exterminator made it up this far. I thought about my pal Conrad and wondered if he'd left the Soviet air base with the rest of the American troops, taking his skills for killing small things back home with him. I fiddled with one of the light bulbs and thought about walking the mile or so down the road for pancakes at a hold in the wall, The Flapjack Shack, that I'd started to frequent when I needed to escape the strip club.

My phone buzzed and pulled it out of my front pocket. The text read: *Stop being a pervert and get your ass to the garage.* Did Bianca have the ability to see me in my perch? The surveillance system that Blake had put in place made me wonder if I was alone anywhere at Club Paradise

I descended to the main club and out the back of the building. This time, there was no Iman or congregation of messed-up hipsters from the afterparty waiting for me. Instead, Deacon was hanging outside the back door with the keys to the town car. The ring looked small in his mammoth hand. Nikki sat in the back seat, dressed in workout clothes, texting on her phone. Something didn't seem right with the bodybuilder. The rings around his eyes were more pronounced than usual. I stepped over to give him a high five but had to act quickly to catch the keys he flung at my chest.

"What do you do exactly?" Deacon asked. "Mitzu and I had a talk. We're now on door duty exclusively, while you get to take everyone to their appointments."

"I have no idea."

Deacon stepped up to me, his mammoth chest blocking Nikki from view.

"Sure you're not banging the boss's daughter or his wife?"

"I'm not that LA," I said jokingly, trying to ease the tension.

He pulled down a pair of shades and looked me in the eyes, and then he took a step back, ran his fingers through his thinning hair, and sighed.

"Damn, man, I'm sorry. I think I might have made a mistake. I kept trying to get Big Z and Malik to invest in a film of me playing an action star."

He flexed his bicep, which rippled like waves rolling into the surf.

"There's a lot you can do in life that doesn't involve being a star."

"It's this damn town. It makes everything look sideways." He turned his head, laughing loudly, a smile returning to his face. "All I want is to be the next Schwarzenegger."

"Be Deacon. You're way cooler than he is."

"You know it," he said, flashing me a grin.

"Dude, they want me around because I'm lost," I said. "Beaten down. Human wallpaper."

"You're selling yourself short." Deacon slapped me on the shoulder and strolled toward his pickup truck in the parking lot.

I wasn't so sure about that. The real problem was that I wasn't selling myself at all. My shoulder stung from the bodybuilder's tap and I fumbled to find the ignition key on the ring.

Nikki looked up from her phone and raised an eyebrow. "C'mon, West, I have needs. Isn't it time you let me know you're the man for the job?"

Errands flew by quickly. A trip to the drug store was followed by a thirty-minute stop at a high-end gym in Beverly Hills. Through the windows, I caught flashes of sculpted bodies spinning on machines. They reminded me of hamsters safe behind the glass, apart from the fury of the world and oblivious to anything outside. The carnage I'd seen on the other side of the world, with prisoners in cages, could never be explained. There was too much distance between the worlds of the rich and the dying.

I finished my paperback, leaving only one novel left in the series. Bored, I flipped through the AM and FM dials. I settled on a sportscaster pontificating on the dramas of sports heroes: stars that smacked around their kids and significant others. It had probably always been the case, but social media and cellphones had made it easy to capture people behaving badly. I idled the engine in the red zone to keep the AC running and waited. Nikki returned, jumped into the back seat, and ordered me to crank up the tunes. She directed me to some pop station as I pulled out into traffic. Nikki lounged in the back of the car, running her fingers through her wet hair and punching away at cell phone. I tried to not watch in the rearview mirror and instead set my mind on getting her to her shift at the Hair Empire.

I stopped at a light, waiting for it to turn green. A mother carrying several full canvas bags headed toward me, a young girl, barely old enough to stand upright, in tow. Even though the "do not walk" light was blinking the countdown, the woman cut across the intersection and strolled as though she had all the time in the world, with the little girl struggling to keep up. The light turned green when they were halfway across. The traffic remained paused in the other lane waiting for them to move past. Car horns from both directions blared. I found myself seeing red. I pulled up behind them and screeched to a stop, unrolling my window.

"You're putting your daughter's life at risk, you selfish asshole!" I screamed, and the woman turned around. Instead of grabbing her daughter's hand, she shot me the bird, spun, and moved even more slowly to the curb, the girl scampering behind her. .

"Jesus, West, that's some serious losing your shit! You're not a robot after all."

My hands were shaking as I accelerated back into traffic. "I'm not sure your mother would agree."

"She does like telling you what to do," Nikki admitted. "It's because she feels helpless in her own house."

"And you're the prisoner in the tower," I said.

"Disney gets it wrong. The evil mother isn't always a bad thing. Sometimes she has to be more of a monster than the father is just to get by."

"Exactly how bad is it to live with Big Z?" I asked.

"Enough for me to plan my exit strategy."

Strange how the language of relationships can mimic that of

war. The traffic was starting to jam up from morning rush hour. I found myself checking each intersection for kids.

Nikki continued. "As bad as it is for me, it's a billion times worse for my mom."

"She seems pretty tough to me."

"It's funny. In a town full of wannabe stars, the best actresses are the ones in abusive relationships."

Wealth alone didn't protect you from the bad men of the planet. Neither did being one yourself.

During my lunch run for the Hair Empire staff, I dropped by the used bookstore. The owner had taken a liking to me and had kept an eye out for Travis McGee novels. He handed me a copy of *The Lonely Silver Rain.* and asked me who my next author would be. I told him that I couldn't plan that far ahead.

I sat on a bench outside the Hair Empire and ate a chicken sandwich and began to read the first chapter of the novel. I'd spent more than twenty novels with a man who tried to do the right thing but continually faced monsters in the shape of men. Travis McGee would know what to do about a man like Big Z. Maybe I should follow his example. The detective had lost lovers and friends and more lovers. He let money slip through his fingers. He let the scars build up but it didn't seem to make him tougher. I worried that this final book would kill him.

Jesus, here I was worrying about a fictional character. What was wrong with me? Donya popped outside and scooted onto the bench beside me, lighting up a smoke. After growing up around gamblers and serving a stint in the military, I found the scent of cigarettes comforting. Pops, in particular, liked to drive with the windows up while he sucked on the cancer sticks. He was too cheap to let the AC out along with the smoke, even when I complained. Donya shot me a sidelong glance, took a drag, and cleared her throat.

"Weather doesn't change much here," I said in a halfhearted attempt at small talk.

"People don't change much either."

Donya blew a smoke ring, a nice wide one, something I'd only ever seen a few women do. The O wobbled before splitting apart to join the waves of other gray in the sky.

"The Pouralis are Iranian Jews. Do you know what that means?"

"That you have a chip on your shoulder?"

"Exactly," Donya said. "We've been looking over our shoulders since we've had shoulders. We tend to rub people the wrong way."

"Sounds like my family."

"Some people call my brother a bad guy, but he's a teddy bear at heart."

I couldn't help but think of the march of teddy bears at Club Paradise, an event that took place every night. It wasn't enough to get the customers to spend ridiculous amounts on tips and lap dances. Big Z also had a collection of teddy bears and other stuffed animals that he bought wholesale. They were then brought out, one per dancer, in a march around the club with a price tag of twenty bucks a piece. They sold. Almost all of them. Every time. I wondered how many kids got those presents from absentee dads, and how many wives had a temporary reprieve from wondering where their men had been.

"Big Z scares a lot of people," I said. "The dancers. His employees. Maybe even his family."

Donya became visibly upset. She stubbed out her cigarette on the bench arm and let it fall to the ground. "That bitch Bianca is poisoning you; I can tell."

"I can make up my own mind."

"Look, that man has gone through hell with that woman. And his daughter is an ungrateful little tramp. You steer clear of both. They'll turn you inside out and your life will be over before you understand how it happened."

"Thanks for the warning," I said.

Donya shook her head. "I know what you're really saying is *fuck off* old woman. My brother isn't perfect, but he's sacrificed a lot to put a roof over our heads. Don't think it doesn't hurt him when others in our community look down on him for the business he runs."

"Yeah, he's some Good Samaritan."

"He took you in. Don't forget that. He has flaws, sure, but he's does what he does to protect his family."

And to get young strippers to sleep with him. This time, though, I kept my thoughts to myself. I looked straight ahead and nodded until Donya left, until I was staring at the muddled horizon in hopes I might finally see the blue sky. When my eyes grew tired of staring out into the void, I opened my paperback and began to read.

I dropped off Nikki at UCLA campus for her summer course, a German class. She was taking a year to decide what she wanted to do with her life. My own college fund had, so far, gone unused. Someday I would need to run toward a solution and not away. I decided to take a jog. I ran through the heart of UCLA campus as though my life depended on it. I got more than a few looks because I was wearing black slacks and a black T-shirt along with my black tennis shoes. It wasn't exactly a jogging outfit. I'm not sure when yoga pants replaced jeans and why women of all sizes decided to wear them, but it distracted me during my first attempt at exercise in more than a week. I covered a couple of miles, weaving around kids with backpacks and late-model luxury sedans gliding through campus. I made sure to follow the law when crossing the street in case some gung-ho campus cop was on duty. Being AWOL made me think about the law more than I ever had as an MP.

I was dying for water, so I completed my circuit back to Nikki's building and headed inside to find a water fountain. I found one next to a glass case with a map and photos from student trips to Germany. A ring of sweat had formed on my T-shirt and it made me self-conscious.

There were students around and they were mostly my age. Why then did I consider them kids? My own maturity was seriously in doubt after going AWOL. I'm sure those students also had problems, but I assumed, somehow, that they had parents who cared and were looking out for them. That just pissed me off—it was stupid to feel sorry for myself. The door to a conference hall swung open and Nikki was one of the first to emerge, instantly taking my arm in hers.

"Ewww, you're all wet," she said, before leaning in and whispering in my ear, "and so am I."

I ignored the flirtation, obviously provided for shock value, and tried to steer us toward the parking garage. Nikki took hold of my arm and yanked me in the exact opposite direction. She seemed to be in a much better mood now that she was done with work and school.

"Where are we headed?" I asked.

"Someplace beautiful. You'll see."

"I'm not sure your parents would like us hanging out like this."

"My mom knows I like you. As far as my dad is concerned…I don't care if he fucking drops dead. The asshole."

"Hey, look, I understand being mad at your father. Mine was no prize. When he was gone, though, I felt a little differently."

Nikki's face burned with an emotion I didn't recognize. We passed several women her age, all of them blond.

"Not me. Mom and I are prisoners. Dad's made both of us do things. Sick things to show he's the big man in the family"

If Big Z was abusive, it would explain the secret note, the whispers, the hints.

"You're over eighteen. I left home when I was your age. You have choices."

"Not without money I don't. I've got a plan to get some though."

"I bet you do," I said.

"Don't be nasty. I'm not like one of those club hos pulling tricks."

"Some of them are nice," I said. "Like Alice."

"She's a different brand of crazy," Nikki agreed, veering us off the main path to a more secluded path away from the road.

"You sure you don't want your folks to pay for your school?" I asked. "It's just a few more years."

"It's a trap. If I stay, I'll never get away. I know it. I'm going to let you in on a secret."

"You're crazy about me?" I asked.

"That's no secret. I'm learning German so I can run off to school in Berlin next year. It's free for American students. I just need the cash to travel and to get an apartment there.

"Sounds like it could be a learning experience," I said.

"You could always join me."

"Sure," I said jokingly, but she slid her arm down to squeeze my hand in a long painful grip. It was a strange way to hold hands and her fingernails dug into my palms.

"We're here. I have something to show you."

She let go of my hand and gestured at the entrance to the botanical gardens. We slid through an archway with a ticket booth at the end. I felt skittish about strolling through a garden with my boss's daughter and felt even less sure when I was tugged toward a family bathroom. She eyed the bored ticket taker carefully before opening the door and pulling me inside. She locked it behind her and pressed up against me. There was no place for me to retreat, no place to hide.

"So," she said, gesturing to the mirror. "Aren't I beautiful? I promised I'd show you something."

"Yes," I said in the automatic reply that men have provided to crazy women since the beginning of time.

Nikki smiled and took off her top and bra. Her shoes and yoga pants followed, leaving her in light blue socks and nothing else. Her nipples were erect and small, and her pubic hair was shaved, a look that always made me feel uncomfortable.

I was already hard by the time she unzipped my trousers and took my cock into her mouth. Yes, this is actually happening to you. Yes, you should not be doing this. Yes, you should ask about birth control before leaning her over the sink. No, you should not look at yourself in the mirror while driving yourself into this woman from behind. Yes, you are quickly tipping over the edge. No, you don't feel like slowing down and savoring the moment. Yes, you pull out and spray your semen all over the baby changing station. No, you cannot bring yourself to say anything at all as you try to clean yourself up, wipe down the mess, hold yourself together.

It was sunset by the time I dropped off Nikki and the car and got back to Club Paradise. The twin towers of the faux castle hung above the Far Horizon warehouse. The almost-full moon was cradled between them, the way my head had rested between Nikki's breasts until a knock at the door prompted us to put our clothes back on. She had been distant on the way home, texting on her phone. We didn't speak a single word during the drive.

I was confused about our relationship and could sense the stupidity of my actions. Big Z might not kill me for dating his daughter, but he sure as hell could put a world of hurt on me given the rough crowd of people in his employ and those on the periphery of his dealings. It was rumored that he got his liquor at cut-rate prices from a dicey distributor with criminal ties and liked to pal around with a crooked fight promoter.

Big Z was still a mystery to me. I only saw him in small doses, hitting the floor for a few minutes to talk up the regulars or to pick up one of the dancers to spend the night in the apartment above his office. The girls, for the most part, refused to talk about him. Although, if I had to guess, almost all of them had slept with him. There was still a lot about the man and his family that I didn't understand. Maybe I could be like the detective in the novel. Maybe I could do some good for Nikki and her mother.

A murdered-out black SUV idled in the parking lot as I turned the corner. The sound of laughter rose above the engine and a hooded figure was silhouetted in the dim light. It was Ricki Ticki. He was smoking a joint. Far as I knew, he was still banned from the premises.

I wasn't looking to surprise the creep. I made sure to circle around so that Ricki could see me coming before approaching his window. His smile only grew bigger when he saw me heading his way. The dude had the stones to air-kiss me, his lips smacking, smoke rising, driver's side window rolling up. If he thought glass separating us was going to matter, he had another thing coming. I envisioned the punch before I threw it and shortened my steps as I approached. Luckily for the hooded drug dealer, a familiar figure got out of the passenger's door. Solomon held a paper bag with one hand and with the other he made the universal stop signal, flat palm outward.

"Hold up a sec," Solomon said.

"Hey, man, what the hell is going on?" I asked.

The car window whirred down a few inches and a voice cackled, "I'll let you two girls sort this out."

"Yeah, you better run," I yelled.

The car tires spun, leaving rubber on the pavement, the scent of gas fumes and marijuana floating into the evening sky above us.

Solomon shuffled over and rested a hand on my shoulder. "C'mon, let's go inside."

I stepped away and slapped at the paper bag, feeling out of the loop, betrayed, scared for my dumbass friend.

"What the hell's this? Dealing could get you jail time. Could get you killed."

"Look, I know the risks. From using. From hooking up people here at the club. For getting myself tangled with the Pouralis. You're the one with your head up your ass, though."

"How do you figure? When's the last time you had a full night of sleep?"

"I'm not sticking it to the boss's daughter for starters."

"Hey, I've got things under control."

"Do you really? Jesus, you're on the run from the military and you're lecturing me."

"Because you need it."

"Buddy, you don't have a fucking clue. I do what I do to have a good time. You do everything out of guilt."

"Not everything. Man, I'm just looking out for you."

Solomon shook his head sadly. "Your parents did a number on you. You know, Lucinda wasn't your fault."

The name struck a chord. I seemed to remember a girl with messy dark hair who used to follow us around.

"What does a neighbor kid have to do with anything?"

This time Solomon put his hand on my shoulder and gripped it hard. "You're not to blame for your sister, okay? You need help. And I can't give it to you. Sorry."

Solomon headed toward the back entrance and I trudged after him like I was wading in water. Each step took forever, and my legs were rubbery. White dots danced in the corners of my eyes. Images from my childhood flashed and I could almost picture a young girl, barely able to walk, always around before she wasn't. My trek through the kitchen and to the bar brought me no closer to understanding. I wanted to ask Solomon what he meant but he disappeared into the dancers' dressing room.

Malik emerged from a seat by the main stage and took my elbow. "West, you need to keep an eye on your boy. He's messing up. He's late. Again."

"I don't get it. He doesn't start DJing until later."

"Don't be stupid. You're not *that* guy. He has responsibilities. I need you to make sure he delivers on them. If he doesn't, I'll hold you responsible."

"I work for your mother," I said.

Malik pulled me close like he was going to kiss me. His pupils were dilated, and he grinned like we were old pals. "You're fucked then."

Malik returned to his seat and snapped his fingers for Flynn to refresh his drink. I was unsteady on my feet, exhausted by the black hole of my childhood memories. Could I really have had a sister I didn't remember? I was barely able to stand. Alice was the only one who noticed my confusion and she ushered me to the door, telling me to *go home and sleep it off*, as if you could sleep off grief. It was only after my walk to the apartment building that I understood that home meant Alice's pad and not

Solomon's. I used her spare key to let myself into her antiseptic apartment.

I lay down on the couch and my phone buzzed. I was too exhausted to deal with Bianca and I was relieved to see that it was Pops. His message was probably full of shit, but to the point: *Come visit us at the L Hotel in Vegas. I think Moms is cheating on me.*

15

DESERT SHADOWS

I'm not sure what the hell these women were thinking? It was hotter than even my hottest day in Afghanistan, well over a hundred degrees and rising. No way, though, was I going to take the bait and suit up. Swimming pools, in general, weren't my thing, and it could turn an already awkward situation even more awkward. I sat in a lawn chair with my back to the house in my club uniform, sweating my balls off and following the slivers of shade so I wouldn't get fried by the sun. I'd brought along my last Travis McGee mystery to read. Not that I could focus. I hoped my sunglasses kept the women, who were splashing in the pool, from noticing that I was watching them. Who could blame me? It was pretty entertaining to check out the two-on-two volleyball competition: Mona and Alice versus Bianca and Nikki.

Yes, it had seemed weird earlier that morning when I'd picked up all four women in the back parking lot of the Far Horizon warehouse. They all looked freshly showered and dressed, and I wondered if they'd finished an aerobics class with Solomon. We hadn't spoken in days. I'd lately taken to watching the door to his place through the half-pulled blinds at Alice's. Alice and I had settled into a domestic routine, with me cleaning and cooking, and Alice retreating to her room for long stretches to chat with her phone psychic. She had problems that ran as deeply as my own. For that reason, I was divided about which team I was routing for. Nikki had my heart but I disliked and mistrusted her mother almost as much as I did my own.

After the two-hour drive out to this private, Palm Springs gated community, they'd invited me to hang in the pool. I decided to play manservant instead. I'd already blended and delivered two pitchers of margaritas to them. The condo was adobe-ranch style, similar to dozens of others in the subdivision. The muted tan colors blended into the hilltops, and the buildings encircled a golf course. One of the Pourali's owned the place, and I couldn't help but notice a Warhol of Bianca over the kitchen table in the dining room. *Girls' weekend* was the answer given to me when I asked how long we would be staying. I hadn't had a chance to pack a change of clothes of my own and was stuck in black slacks and T-shirt. There were loaner swimsuits, of course, but I didn't want to be without my armor. I cooled myself by sucking on ice cubes and the occasional splash of water that reached me from the spirited match.

Women confounded me. I suspected that I never measured up to their expectations of what I could be and the reality of who I actually was. Mom's disappointment had been clear to me from my earliest memories. I think it wired me to seek approval from the women in my life. Like with Moms, the more I tried to please them, the harder they pushed me away.

It wasn't just me, though. Pops, too, seemed to come up short of the mark. Their sophisticated scams never quite afforded them the comforts she craved from having grown up dirt-poor in Shreveport. I suspected my parents had always had affairs, but the situation must have been pretty grim for Pops to text me about it. Perhaps betrayal by women was part of the family curse for firstborn sons, a curse that had followed the Rivet men since the end of the Civil War. Since then, we had waged war against everything and everyone and ended up in jail, dead, hated, and forgotten by all but the next hapless generation.

"Match point, bitches," Bianca yelled.

"Bring it, bitches," Mona hollered back.

The contest had been tied at one game apiece and it looks like the rubber match had grown vicious. All of the women were good athletes, and the smack talk was constant and impressive. Nikki and Alice were both tall, just short of model height but rangy enough to spike over the net stretched across the pool. Bianca and Mona were as competitive as two sisters-in-law could be, barking out orders, digging out balls, and serving to the other. The pool wasn't more than four feet deep where they played, splaying out on either end into a circular deep end joining at a rock waterfall. Bianca served for match point and Mona hit a soft return to the right side. Nikki leaped but the ball spun over her fingers. Bianca raced to the edge of the pool and dove, the ball smacking against her fist. The ball spun crosscourt, and Alice dove sideways and hit into the net. Bianca's momentum, though, carried her into the turquoise tile and she yelped. A gash had opened on her arm and I raced over the see if she was okay. She didn't care that she was in pain, only that she and Nikki had won.

The first aid kit was the largest I'd ever seen— a bulky metal kit the size of a briefcase. It was well-stocked but had seen some use before. I found it under the sink in the master bathroom. Bianca, uncharacteristically, followed my lead when I suggested she follow me inside to bandage her wound. Her forearm was scraped badly, and the gouge running forearm to elbow bled in intermittent spots. After disinfecting her arm with Bactine, it took me several gauze bandages to stop the bleeding.

"Will there be any scarring?" Bianca asked.

"No, I think it should be okay," I said.

"You're a strange bird." Bianca ran her fingers along the bandages. "Do I need any stitches?"

"No, not for a wound like this."

"Seems like you might be speaking from experience." Bianca ran her index finger along the white lines of healed scars that crisscrossed my arm, battle tattoos dished out by Moms, often with a wooden spoon. Pops was the one who'd take me to the bathroom afterward, patch me up, and chew me out for not backing down when she was in one of those moods.

"We all have our problems," I said.

"Some larger than others. You look like you've seen a few battles."

Again, the hints about my past. "I guess it's in my nature to look after folks."

"Do I look like someone who needs looking after?" Bianca asked.

"Maybe."

"And Nikki?"

"Definitely."

"You think you're the man to do it?" she asked. Even though her tone was teasing I wasn't going to rise to the bait.

"You pay me to be the man to do it."

"That's what I want to hear," Bianca said, standing up from her perch on the closed toilet seat and marching out of the bathroom. "We'll see how far you're willing to go."

I'm not sure why but my hands were shaking when I threw the wrappers in the trashcan and returned the items to the kit. There was a needle and thread there alongside the salves, itch creams, and painkillers. The only time Moms looked at my injuries was after she threw a pan at me and caused a gash on my temple. The wound wouldn't stop bleeding.

Pops wanted to take me to the doctor, but Moms shook him off. She boiled water and sterilized a needle. She spooled black thread expertly through the eye and told me I would regret it if I flinched. One of the few things Moms spoke about from her own childhood was how she'd sewn every stitch of clothing for herself. because her own mother was too poor to buy clothes. I didn't remember my grandmother on either side as they'd both died when I was young. I looked Moms in the eyes as she expertly applied stitches, her face radiant. It was seared into my memory, that moment, because normally her look was one of disgust. It was in that rare glimpse, I could see why so many people fell to her charms.

Muted laughter drifted through the house but for some reason, it felt foreboding. The afternoon sun cast shadows of the ants that scurried along the bathroom windowsill. I felt like killing them, but it seemed too petty. I wanted to escape but there was nowhere I could go. As usual, one of the women in my life beckoned to me, this time Nikki, to make them margaritas. I was frozen, though, unable to move until a lithe form came back to the bathroom to find me.

"We all want you to come into the other room to service us." Nikki kissed me on the lips and slapped me on the ass. Some of us more than others."

"Why did I lose?" I asked Alice, after helping her get out of her jeans and into bed. She was obviously drunk, and I hid her phone so she couldn't call one of her favorite phone psychics.

"Bullshit is a bullshit card game," she said, slapping the bed for me to join her. I shook my head. I'd agreed to sleep in Alice's room tonight because they were one bedroom short, but I'd already decided I would stretch out on the reclining chair by the door, which I left slightly ajar.

"If that was true, I wouldn't have lost every hand," I said.

"You're just no damn good at lying," she said.

"Maybe all I need is practice," I suggested.

"Iranian women are born lying as a way to deal with the fucking patriarchy. Mona and Nikki probably don't know how to tell the truth."

"Hey, that's not cool."

Outside, in the hallway, I heard soft footsteps approach the door and stop.

"Don't get PC on me, kiddo. It doesn't suit you. And Bianca always told the biggest whoppers in my family, at holidays, re-unions, hell any time I saw her."

"What are you talking about, Alice?"

"We're cousins, you idiot. Why do you think I get treated different than the other dancers? Bianca thinks I'm her eyes and Big Z thinks I'm his pimp, picking out girls for him. Truth is I'm both and I deserve every second of this bullshit life I'm living."

"What the hell happened to you, Alice? Why are you so god-damned sad all the time?"

"Every dancer is sad," she said.

"Don't avoid the question."

"My boy is dead, okay? I let him run out into the street to chase a soccer ball. I was distracted. I was a horrible mother and I'm just like the creature in the horror movie I'm playing. Only thing is that I'm deadlier."

I sat down beside her and held her close to me, but I felt like a hand was pulling at me from the grave, like there was nothing separating Alice from me in our cursed existences.

That night, I dreamed that an old woman in a white dress entered the room. She was nearly translucent, and her face was thin, almost elf-like. I couldn't exactly stare through her. It was as though I could look into her. She was smiling at me, but I was terrified. As she moved toward me, I had time to etch every detail in that room in my brain. The lines in the ceiling that weren't unlike the scars on my body. The wood paneling, which was warped from time and the buckling of the building to the wind and sun. The wrinkles in the gaunt face framed by white hair. The outline of Alice in the bed next to me as she huddled with the sheet pulled around her. *Wake up*, I told myself. That did not stop the ghost from climbing on top of me, from cupping my face.

With extreme effort, I pulled myself out of the dream. I found myself shivering; the T-shirt and board shorts I'd borrowed to sleep in were soaked in perspiration. I slipped out of the chair, weak in the knees, and stumbled out into the living room.

I drank a glass of water and lay down on the sofa, waiting for the dawn to break. I closed my eyes. I'd heard that during meditation some people found a realm that was calming, a safe place where they could strengthen themselves from the inside out. Whenever I tried to let my thoughts drift into nothingness, I found myself floating in a cold dark river. There was something lost beneath the water, something beckoning me to follow. I could almost feel this other presence pressed up to me through the blackness. I could almost feel something that I'd lost.

I opened my eyes and found Mona straddling me in the near darkness, sunrise slicing the sky and casting her face in a horrifying half-smile. She was dressed in underwear and T-shirt, and I could feel her compact and muscular body pressed against me. I wanted to throw her off me but I was paralyzed. I could understand how Solomon could risk so much for the chance to have her pull him into her.

"I thought you were a ghost."

"You saw her?" Mona asked.

"Yes, a thin woman with white hair. She was beautiful and terrifying."

"Iman and Malik have seen her too. But no one else. None of the women. She used to own this place with her husband, at least that's what we've been told by the caretaker."

"I don't believe in ghosts," I said.

"That doesn't matter when they believe in you. The woman was an actress who married a TV producer. He made dozens of pilots, but none of them ever saw the light of day."

"Why did she appear to me?"

"Maybe she wanted to cheat on her husband with a younger man but never had the nerve. I'm not going to die with those kinds of regrets."

"What about Solomon?"

"What about him? He's playing a dangerous game."

"What is he doing for you?"

"Keep your voice down. What isn't he doing? He's dealing drugs to the dancers and customers at the club for Malik. He's providing Goddess Guides with a feel-good vibe. He's using the products himself and becoming unreliable."

I shifted myself into a sitting position, causing Mona to slide off my chest so that we were sitting side by side.

"Jesus, you only have to know Solomon for fifteen minutes to understand that he's not reliable."

"That doesn't cut it. He's dealing with people who have very little patience. All the Pouralis have a cut of the action, including me. All of them are greedy. None of them tolerate failure."

"This sounds like a warning."

"I can see now that your innocent act isn't really an act. I can see why Nikki's hot for you. You better tell Solomon to get his shit together or he's going to find himself kissing the dirt instead of me."

I wanted to ask her what she knew about my relationship with Nikki, but all I could think about was how much trouble my oldest friend was in. Solomon was on a collision course with his own nature and the unforgiving underbelly of Los Angeles. The castles of that town were built on sweat equity that had soaked into the parched earth. Mona kissed me gently on the cheek and laughed at the bulge in my shorts. She padded back to her room, and I huddled in the corner of the couch, watching the sky slowly peel back its eyelids.

All four women sat together at the dining room table, all of them obviously hungover. Conversation, at first, was sparse. They held their heads and looked at their tiny screens, the new version of a newspaper. I cleared away the card deck and wine glasses from the night before and set the table for breakfast. Alice must have felt bad for how much I was doing and told me to chill. She went into the kitchen to make us coffee and start cracking eggs for omelets. I still felt uncomfortable and hovered in the doorway.

Mona and Bianca began chatting about how it had been the right move to leave their husbands at home. I was about to head into the kitchen to see if I could help Alice when Nikki rose from her chair and clutched my elbow. She steered me down the hallway to the back door and we ducked off into a small room with nothing more than a desk, a couch, and a TV with VCR. Above the desk were videos of TV pilots, with faded labels written in block letters in barely legible black ink.

"A producer lived here before us. With his wife. Apparently, she died here from a drug overdose, and he disappeared."

"He went on the run?"

"No, his car was still here. Some people think he went out

into the desert and died from grief. Do you want to know what
I think?"

Nikki took one of the pilots, titled *Father Knows Best*, out of
its cardboard sleeve. She slipped it into the ancient VCR and
flicked on the TV.

"Always," I said.

She nodded for me to sit on the couch, and I obliged. She
joined me, remote in hand, sliding in next to me so that our
hips touched.

"I think the woman killed her fucking asshole of a husband
and dumped him in the desert. Then had the best sleep of her
life. The sleep of the dead."

"I saw her ghost," I said.

The credits for the pilot rolled and Nikki gripped my hand
tightly.

"Of course you did. You're never far from your ghosts.
That's what I like about you."

"How do you know about my past?"

"Solomon told me, of course. Where do you think my
friends get their pot?"

I was torn by several conflicting emotions. Interested that
Nikki wanted to know more about me. Confused about why
all the Pourali women were digging into my past. Scared about
what they and I would discover if we dug too deeply.

"This pilot really pisses me off. I watch it to remind myself
that this shit shouldn't happen."

The pilot followed the story of a husband and wife with two
daughters, set during the late 1960s. The wife was portrayed as
a liberal and the girls as budding hippies, but all of them got
into trouble, only to be rescued by their cigar-smoking father
who was also an advertising man. It felt like *Bewitched*, only there
was no magic in the world, except that of men looking to their
grind butts and their womenfolk beneath the shoes that were
shined for them. All the women had reluctant smiles for Father,
but their eyes told a different story. They reminded me of the
dancers' eyes.

Nikki slipped her hand into the front pocket of my pants and pulled out my phone. She examined the screen, and I wondered if she was scanning my texts. She placed herself in my contacts and sent herself a text from my phone, filled with emoticon hearts and kisses. She slipped the device back into my pants and gave my hand a squeeze.

"Breakfast is ready," Alice called. "Let's get a good meal before we head out,"

Nikki jumped up from the couch and streaked into the hallway. I returned the tape to its place among the other pilots that had never seen the light of day outside this room. It struck me then that the mother in the show had been a younger version of the ghost I'd seen. The actress who'd owned this place. The shade of a woman who still inhabited these walls. Maybe she'd been trying to tell me something. Like the fortune teller I'd met before my flight back to the states. I needed to navigate the dead zone, to dart between cactuses that threw shadows like people and away from people that cast shadows like animals.

16

TWIN SHADOWS

Solomon was the brother I never had. He was Huck and Tom rolled into one, and I was his faithful bodyguard. We got into a lot of scrapes, leaving Solomon with bravado and me with scars. We spent nearly every waking moment together, hanging out in each other's homes until our home life fell apart and we both became interested in girls. We were still brothers, but our private language was fractured and would never recover. I felt closer to him than my fast-talking folks, moody girlfriend, and even the twin I'd absorbed. Solomon and I had spent most of our lives being each other's shadows. Now it felt like he was trying to escape me.

To be fair, Solomon didn't like being called on his shit. Who does, I guess? He didn't want to untangle himself from seeing a married woman and slinging dope, that much was clear. He was an adrenaline junkie, a guy who enjoyed walking the razor's edge. Usually, these problems went away by moving around on our yearly exodus with the other *Aces* families. Maybe this was why Solomon never learned his lesson. He just started over in a different city. I'd suggested as much on the night I got back from Palm Springs, and he got pissed and accused me of wanting what was his. I turned my back on him, gathered the rest of my things, and moved into Alice's place for good. I didn't want to have *his* life. Why couldn't he see it? I wanted him to have *a* life.

Nikki told me to let him cool off. We were on UCLA campus, and we were brazenly holding hands. We endd up back in the unisex bathroom at the botanical gardens after I drove her to her weekly German class. This time I had a condom. Afterward, she gave me advice about my oldest friend while she texted her friends. I was still unsettled by how often she looked at her phone. Who was I to judge, though? She had started to text me more often since the trip out to the desert, more than her mother, more than my cryptic Pops. She told me that I needed to start looking for what came next for me. I hadn't told her I was a man on the run. I didn't have to. You didn't end up at a place like Club Paradise unless you'd run out of options.

It was dusk by the time I dropped Nikki off. I'm not sure if Bianca was peeved that I got her home late, but she texted me to cover security on the night shift at the club. Sleep was overrated anyway. I got precious little of it. Perhaps the genesis was the countless hours I'd spent on the night shift in Bagram guarding prisoners, a zombie version of myself rereading Deirdre's letters, or shooting the shit with Niles about obscure films or underappreciated authors. Staying up until sunrise was something I did regularly at Club Paradise, shuffling along the crannies and corridors even when I was off shift, avoiding real problems and real relationships.

Tonight was busier than usual—the beeps of the machine used to turn credit cards into cash mashed with the overloud music. With more guys came more bad behavior. Deacon, usually annoyingly upbeat, was in a real pisser of a mood. He threatened a half-dozen guys pawing at the dancers, and I could tell that he was eager to toss one of them outside and into orbit. Maybe Deacon was mad that I was no longer working the door regularly, or that I was the one who'd accompanied Malik earlier that evening on a trip to the liquor store to snag a couple of high-end bottles of Scotch for a bachelor party in the VIP room.

I asked Malik about Solomon and he told me that it looked like he'd gone AWOL. I'm not sure why he used a military expression. It seemed out of context and I wondered how close Bianca was to her son. I imagined the Pouralis maneuvered through their lives a bit like contestants on *Survivor*, in a constant battle of trying to build alliances. The tension, at times, erupted beneath the surface and the aftershocks could be felt throughout the club. There was no escaping conflict, no matter where I ran.

Working in a strip club reminded me of the army. You get numb to men behaving badly and civility melting away. The impersonal nature of the interactions fed some reptilian center of the brain. The men there, except for Blake, showed no compassion or tenderness for the dancers. The fog of liquor and drugs hung in the air to give cover like a smoke grenade in the field, but it did not stop you from seeing too much. This act of witnessing changed you, even if you didn't participate. If darkness needed to be fed to survive, then Club Paradise was the machinery fueling it.

Something was brewing in the club. When Alice was on stage, a clean-cut man with a blond buzz cut and powder blue suit followed behind her on her circuit while she danced. He looked out of place. Alice went out of her way to flirt, uncharacteristically, with the other men surrounding her, except for the guy trying so hard to get her attention. Blake, ex-spook that he was, tracked this from his seat at the bar and grew more agitated as the night progressed. Just before closing time, he slammed his fist on the counter and stomped over to confront Alice's stalker. The dude was big across the shoulders and looked like an athlete. I stepped over to try to separate them, but Alice beat me to it. She leaned down and flipped a customer's drink in the man's face.

"Just stop it, Alicia!" the man cried out. "Come home."

"I am home," she said, gyrating her way toward the onlookers gripping dollar bills like bus tickets to heaven. "I'm in hell."

The stranger shoved Blake into the wall and bolted outside before I could grab him. I considered following him to make sure he got the message, but Deacon stopped me at the door.

"It's her old man, some Mormon dude from Utah. He comes here every few months to try to get her back."

"We're all living in hell," I muttered, and Deacon flashed his best actor's smile.

Flynn was giving me the cold shoulder, I suppose, because he associated me with Solomon. He'd been a dervish all night, alternating between bartending and DJing. He didn't much like having to cover both jobs and he bad-mouthed Solomon to the regulars. Part of me wanted to stand up for my friend and say that this wasn't something he normally did. But that wouldn't be true. This was par for the course. What was different this time was the number of scary individuals he was pissing off. Including me. Being his babysitter was a thankless task. This time, maybe he needed to get his act together on his own. Maybe he needed to learn that actions had consequences.

Instead of rolling back to the apartment complex to warn Solomon, I decided to hang in the basement with the regulars. They were shooting a replacement scene that hadn't gone well. Alice was dressed normally now or the LA definition of it, in a dress that accentuated her bare arms and legs. She was still a bit crazy-eyed from the scene with her ex earlier in the evening. Blake gave instructions, moving her to the correct spot. The trick was to make it appear that she was having a conversation with the siren version of herself. Watching these scenes was even spookier than the previous ones when she'd been in her black makeup and costume.

Flynn was antsy, trying to speed along the proceedings. He was already paying an editor to finish a rough cut of the film and he needed the footage. He tapped his foot and wrote notes in a dog-eared version of the script. Nothing was going to make Spokane move any quicker. For each shot, he played with the lighting, setting up the camera at a glacial speed. Salt looked jealous of the attention the camera was getting and kept dipping into a stash of donuts, her nervous energy raising the tension further. Irv was the only one who seemed to be enjoying himself, letting Judd apply his makeup and sharing backstage tales of a former era. Finally, Spokane got the shot he was looking for, and pointed his finger for Alice to begin.

The dialogue was okay, I suppose. Not the worst I'd ever heard. Alice delivered fervent pleas to her absent doppelgänger to stop taking revenge against everyone in her life. This was, of course, everyone in the movie. Irv's death scene had been particularly inspired; the siren had plunged a four-inch stiletto heel into his ear after he'd cheated on her. Alice was normally compelling, but tonight she delivered her lines with an urgency and mania that made me feel like I was watching a human car wreck.

After several takes, Spokane broke down the lighting and Flynn sent me upstairs to make more coffee for the crew. They were all in between inebriation and hungover, and cranky. They were also picky and wanted espresso instead of coffee from the machine in the kitchen, which meant using the espresso machine in Big Z's office. Unsure whether he was in the apartment above, I tiptoed to the counter where he kept the machine, unplugged it, and took it to the kitchen. Making each order took time, and after a while, Flynn came upstairs to check on me.

"What's taking so long, dummy?" he asked.

"Damn settings are getting the better of me," I said.

Flynn put his hand on my shoulder. "Sorry, man, I'm a little stressed. I've borrowed money from an old college roomie, an actor, to give a screening of the movie He's going to expect me to pay him back whether we sell it or not."

"There's always a price to pay," I said, which reminded me of Solomon's absence.

"True." Flynn put the coffees on a tray and turned to go.

"Do you think guys like Big Z ever pay a price?" I said.

"Karma's a bitch, but she sleeps with everyone," he said, before making his way to the basement door and disappearing.

Sometimes our actions follow us through one life and sometimes into the next.

Lack of sleep caught up with me, and the next day when I went to pick up Nikki from a sleepover at her friend Betsy's home in Beverly Hills, I drove sluggishly. There were clouds in the sky, and the air smelled like rain, like a cleansing might be coming. When I arrived at the house, I noticed several private security vehicles and I had no doubt my license plate was being captured.

The top floor of the house was barely visible behind a massive gate, and I'd learned in my short time in LA that the best digs were the ones you couldn't see from the street. I texted Nikki that I'd landed, and she slipped out through the gate, barefoot and carrying a pair of heels in her hands, her muscular legs rippling below where her lime-green dress stopped midthigh. Her face was flushed, and I wondered if she was high. I got out of the driver's seat and opened the back door, but instead of getting in, she threw her arms around me. She kissed my neck and whispered, "Don't forget the car is bugged. No need to let anyone know I'm fucking you."

"Is that what we're doing?" I asked.

"Among other things."

"How many secrets are you keeping from your folks?"

"From my mother, teenager stuff. From my father every single fucking thing that matters."

"I don't know what the hell I'm doing," I said.

"Poor baby," she said, tracing her nails along my back, releasing a knot of tension and melting me to the core. "I'll do the planning for both of us."

My hands remained at my side. I felt frozen, unable to move, unable to voice my catalog of worries. If I started, I felt as though I'd never stop. Should we be hugging in public? Shouldn't I turn myself into an army base? Why did I keep seeing tiny shadows everywhere I looked? What was I going to do with my parents? Did I know how to love anyone? "Where in the hell is Solomon?"

"What do you mean?" Nikki asked.

"I think he may be dead."

Nikki ordered me to shut up and trust her, and I wasn't sure I had any choice. She made me sit in the passenger's seat and drove us through the streets as though demons were chasing us. The danger felt palpable. She sped through stop signs and yanked turns at red lights without slowing down. We ended up in Culver City, a neighborhood that looked like it had been stapled onto the west side from some other city. The commercial district was filled with warehouses that had been refurbished into offices and bars. The neighborhood was set into hills that existed in few places south of the valley. A metro stop was under construction and the vibe felt transitory. It wasn't long before we reached a small art gallery called *BAM*.

After Nikki parked the car, she hurried out and I raced to catch up.

"BAM spells out the initials of the owners," Nikki said over her shoulder.

"Who's that?"

"Aren't you reading detective novels? You tell me."

"Bianca, Alice, and Mona."

"That's right, hot shot. Bianca paints, Alice makes jewelry, and Mona shellacs distressed furniture with collages. And it's off-limits to the men in the family," Nikki said.

"Like Hair Empire?" I asked.

"Yes, Big Z and Yar are in massive debt. The female Pouralis all are trying our best to hedge our bets. Everything's being held together by smoke and glue."

"What does that even mean?" I paused at the entrance to the gallery, not sure if I was up for whatever Nikki had in mind.

"It means our whole family is a real shit show right now. Even with this money-laundering scheme." Nikki led me into a nearly empty storefront with three adjacent studios, two on each side and one in back. Inside the entrance, Alice sat on a stool at the register with her head pressed against her phone. She mumbled and waved when we walked in and I assumed she was on with her psychic, the one addiction I understood. The advice the palm reader had given me had stayed with me over the past couple of months, the belief that a life-changing decision was looming. The dead zone she'd told me I carried was reflected back by the art in the studio tenfold. The charcoal paintings were lifelike except for the eyes, feet, fingers, ears— any appendages were smudged into the rest of the landscape.

The people in the frames were fading into the fabric of the world. The jewelry was composed of necklaces, bracelets, and earrings combining pop art with symbols of the dead. The collages on the distressed furniture were even more disturbing. Chairs, tables, and bureaus danced with images of animals, nature, wartime, and the symbols of air, water, and fire.

Nikki directed me to the studio in the back, where Mona was painting a self-portrait. She was working in red charcoal and smudged her lips on the paper until they resembled two parallel rain clouds filled with blood. Her workbench was cluttered with brushes and giant notebooks, acrylics and watercolors, and pen and ink outlines taped to the wall above her desk. Nikki opened the door for me but hung outside while I entered. I wondered about the money-laundering claim and imagined the cash from Goddess Guides moving through the store. Mona didn't look up but muttered, as though to the air, "Why the hell is West here?"

"He needs our help," Nikki called out from outside the door.

"We all need help," Mona said, looking up from her painting. Her eyes were puffy and red, and she looked at me with an expression somewhere between annoyance and anger.

"Do you know where Solomon is?" I asked.

"Far away from here, I hope. I certainly gave him enough money to get out of town. That kid had a target on his back."

"Do you know where he was going?"

"No, and I'm pissed off. I really love him…as much as I can love a man."

"Sounds like the greatest love story of our time," I said.

"You should leave. Tonight. There's no good ending here for you. Big Z will fuck you up when he finds out about you and Nikki."

"I can take care of myself," I said.

"No, you can take care of everyone but yourself," Mona said. "Big Z takes whatever he thinks is his. Including me. Whenever he wants. There's nothing I can do about it but try to avoid getting in his path."

I thought about Travis McGee and if he would turn tail
when there was a monster like Big Z running around, damaging
people the detective cared about. I wasn't scared of the monster in man form. It was the monsters I couldn't identify, the
shadows dodging every time I turned. And it was there again,
a young girl with a smile on her face, just outside the door. I
rushed past Nikki and Alice and out to the sidewalk.

The girl was gone. Disappeared. There was no one there,
except for a man sitting in a car across the street. It was Alice's
ex, staring at the gallery. The asshole didn't notice, until too late,
that I'd crossed the street. I yanked him out of the car, and my
fists moved with precision. I knew where to aim where it would
hurt without maiming or breaking bones. I was an artist in my
own right. It was one of my better efforts, I thought, until the
screaming women rushed out of the store to stop me.

Maybe I was a shadow. It was possible that the twin I'd absorbed was the real me and this husk of a man I inhabited was
following along, oblivious to the trails of blood. The aftermath
of my beat-down of Alice's husband was fuzzy at best. The
curse was a self-fulfilling shame spiral, where every decision
brought me closer to prison and farther from hope.

Mona and Nikki helped the blubbering man back into his
car, and Alice drove me back to her place.

My hands were still stinging when we arrived, but I ran over to
Solomon's abandoned car and pounded it the hood was a match
for my aching fists, at least. There were some things I could not
destroy. I suddenly felt the weariness of no sleep and a life on
the run.

Alice closed the distance between us and took me by the
crook of the arm like a small child or an elderly grandfather.
"Hey, stop," she said. "We don't want anyone to call the cops."

She hummed a lullaby as she led me up the stairs to her
apartment. Blake was in the kitchen. He turned off a pan and
gathered us into a three-way hug. I clamped onto both of those

fucked-up people as they helped me to the bathroom and bandaged my fingers. I was put into bed and draped with a blanket, even though it was summer and I was drenched to the core.

Alice rubbed my head and said, "Lucinda isn't your fault."

"Who?"

"Your baby sister. Solomon told me how she drowned when you were a boy and how it fucked you up. You weren't old enough to be responsible for her."

A shadow in the corner morphed into a silhouette and I closed my eyes. "I need to keep trying," I mumbled.

"You need to forgive yourself. We met each other for a reason. You need to stop beating yourself up and everyone else around you."

Lucinda. I remembered her. The neighborhood girl who followed Solomon and me everywhere was my sister. My dead sister. My parents had left me in charge of her that day and I'd forgotten her. I knew then that I needed to confront my ghosts. I needed to see Pops and Moms.

17

SHADOWS FROM THE PAST

The next morning Bianca gave me the day off. She grilled me (via text) about it until I told her it was a family problem. Alice didn't even need a reason to help me—she tossed me her keys and let me borrow her minivan for the trip. I ignored a couple of messages from Nikki, wondering if it had been wise to give her my digits in the first place. I wasn't sure what to tell her. It was obvious that I was a fuck up and that she would eventually get frustrated with me. Or I would do something to mess things up in epic fashion. It only made the desire to see her more intoxicating. I hoped a trip to Vegas would help me clear my head.

By mid-morning, I was on the road. It felt weird to be driving in the opposite direction. I'd managed to barely keep myself afloat during my time in LA, and it was clear that Solomon and I were perennially in danger, mostly from ourselves. His curse was women, drugs, and a love of living on the edge. My curse was self-inflicted, apparently. Lucinda was the shadow dance I lived every single day.

My memory of Lucinda was foggy. I pictured her tagging along with me and Solomon, a small figure darting behind us, but I couldn't visualize her face. At that time, we were living in an apartment complex called Shangri-Louisiana situated next to a dirty pond. The ramshackle housing where we and the other *Aces* staff lived was temporary. We tended to move like locusts, from location to location, wearing out our welcome and inevitably stealing away without paying final rent. The places we chose weren't too picky about references and there was *never* enough space indoors.

Almost all my memories were of roaming the neighborhoods like dog packs, kids of different ages in tow. People treated us like a band of small thieves wherever we went. It was true that many of us were more than willing to pocket a thing or two we thought could be pawned, but our real assignment was making our marks in a world too large for us. The kids trailing behind us changed over the years as families filtered in and out, but Solomon and I were the veterans, leading the other kids on half-baked adventures.

We built a fort in the woods near every place we stayed and filled them with junk from the neighborhood. And there was always a lot of junk. Transportation was never an issue when we got older. Solomon begged, borrowed, and stole bikes for our posse, sometimes trading the motley selection of items from the Aces' lost-and-found bin for a wobbly mountain bike. We never wore helmets and were always scraped from either falling off the bikes, swashbuckling with sticks, or mixing it up with the other kids. Solomon was a flashpoint for chaos, and I was his protector, never backing down even when the bruises collected. Our collection of vagabonds disbanded when Solomon discovered girls and pot. We hung out together, but not as a whirling clan of kids. I was still the wingman, the guy who would date the uglier sister, gather the beers for the party, drive because I was sober, and keep everything moving steadily through our chaotic lives.

As I turned off the highway for gas just past the Vegas border, I realized I was in a familiar place. The slot machines in the EZ Mart entertained gamblers either too anxious to begin the bloodletting or those hapless souls hoping for some final redemption before they crossed back over the border. The gambling here was a mechanism to separate fools from their money in a way that Louisiana never quite managed, even with the riverboats and back-alley games.

I pre-paid for thirty bucks of gas and when I opened the minivan door, a surprise was waiting for me. Nikki was kicked back in the passenger's seat, painting her toenails red, cotton balls between her toes. She didn't look up at me and I had no idea how she'd managed to stow away without me noticing. I should have been shocked, but it all seemed to make some sort of sick sense.

"I napped the whole way in the far back seat. You're kind of oblivious," she said, blowing on her toes and flashing me a smile. "You weren't answering my messages, so I decided to come along and see what you were doing. It's your fault, really, for ignoring me."

"Your mother is going to kill me."

"I'd worry more about my father on this one. Don't worry. I'm covering for you."

"For me?" I said, finally climbing into the vehicle and reflexively closing the door in case someone was watching, in case Big Z had contacted the cops.

"Look, when you asked my mom for some time off, I figured something was up. I told her I was hanging out with Betsy and spending the night. You've got nothing to worry about."

"Oh, sure."

"Sometimes you need to imagine the possibilities, West. Sometimes you just need to say what the hell."

"Ok, we're just a guy and his girlfriend on a date across state lines. What could go wrong?"

"You consider me your girlfriend? Sounds like we're getting pretty serious," she teased.

"How the hell did you get in here?" I asked, trying to change the subject.

"I saw you grab the keys from Alice, and I snuck inside."

"How did you see that?"

"Through her kitchen window, of course. I'd snuck over to the apartment building to get some action. I thought it might help clear your head after your freak out yesterday."

"At least I'm not stalking you!"

"A booty call is not stalking, dummy. What's your deal? Don't you like me?"

"I'm an idiot for sleeping with my employer's daughter."

She laughed at me and petted the head of one of the dashboard frogs. "You're a moron. First, you're w-a-a-y too high-strung. Second, the damage has been done. I can tell Daddy anytime how good you gave it to me. You don't have a bit of common sense, do you?"

"No, but I can start right this second. I'm driving you back."

"No, you're not. Not unless you want me to accuse you of kidnapping."

"You wouldn't do that to me," I said.

"Listen up, cowboy. I'll destroy anyone who gets between me and what I want."

"And what do you want?"

"You," she said. "For now."

"Perfect. That makes no sense."

"I make more sense than you. You're going to Vegas, right? Doing some gambling?"

"You could say that."

"Then why don't you just consider me your good luck charm?"

I took in a deep breath and exhaled loudly. "Lord knows I could use one."

I was already in the soup. Was that a saying? I slid the key in the ignition and the minivan trembled. I accelerated slowly onto the interstate, the sun lowering behind me. Nikki kidded me for driving like an old man. True criminals were careful. I could see that now. I couldn't make any mistakes or risk being picked up. Even worse, Big Z could have goons on my tail. Nothing to do now but roll with it. The city of lights pulled me forward. The city where people lost money and lost themselves. The city that was built, seemingly, for me.

I broke the silence by telling her about my kid sister, long since buried, about my folks and the chasm that separated me from them. Nikki was silent, but I talked until we saw the light of a pyramid beam across the sky.

The L was one of the newest breeds of Vegas casino hotels that straddled old town and the strip, promising Mardi Gras every night, the loosest slots, and the most scantily clad waitresses serving hurricanes and mint juleps. The outside of the hotel featured a fountain and dancers in feathers passing out plastic beads to drum up business. Nikki and I each wore them like ID badges and walked along a fake Bourbon Street running in an oval from the front door into a maze of shops, Cajun restaurants, and gaming tables. Women strolled in shops while the men (and hardcore gamblers of both sexes) got lost in the inner circle. Walkways were painted blue like the Mississippi River. Of course, the real river was closer to dark brown. It made complete sense that this half-assed casino would be the type of place my parents would land post resurrection.

We ended up at a bar called Voodoo Lounge and started sucking down hurricanes like any tourist looking to get lubricated out of their savings. The staff jangled by, dressed in jangled beads and uniforms that were so tight they exposed all their major arteries. The drinks were stiff and the infusion of sugar made me realize I hadn't eaten in hours.

A man was across the bar, pale and drunk, the links of dog tags visible beneath a Vegas T-shirt. He stared into his video poker screen with dead eyes. His hair was just beginning to grow out on the sides, and I wondered how long he'd been out of the service. There were countless stories of men returning from combat missions, draining their savings in every conceivable manner, dropping their education funds on online colleges looking to squeeze them into a half-assed dream of normalcy. The injuries weren't always visible. The lack of concern for personal safety was a way to engage the adrenaline, to trick the heart back into action, to turn today into a possible tomorrow.

I stuffed a twenty into Nikki's video poker machine, inset into the bar. This was a game she knew. She gambled while we both talked shit about our parents. Our stories couldn't have been any different. My folks had imposed no structure while Nikki's kept close tabs, treating her like a Disney princess complete with guards and a tower.

"My mother has bruises all over her arms, every day. It's why she almost never leaves the house," Nikki said.

"She should consider bolting then."

"Dad's made it clear divorce isn't an option."

"What exactly does she think he'll do?"

"Almost anything. That's something we Pouralis have in common when we're threatened."

My focus shifted to Nikki and the watchdog in me snapped to attention. Looking after others—Solomon, prisoners, dancers, Nikki—was my addiction, my way of trying to keep the panic inside from taking hold, to keep control in the chaos of my life, to make me feel better about the loss of Lucinda.

I felt the need to talk, and Nikki was a surprisingly good listener, given what a pain she was most of the time we were together.

"My father made threats, too, all the time. I got my fair share of beatings. After a while there was no sense fighting the schemes he cooked up," I admitted.

"At least you spent time with your father."

"Only when there was something in it for him. He even had his own motive for teaching me to drive in the parking lot of a Walmart when I was fifteen."

"I still don't have a license," Nikki complained, trying to draw two cards on an inside straight, a sucker move.

"My first license wasn't even real. Pops and my uncle wanted me to help run liquor to dry counties, so he got me my first fake ID. I assume he knew that I would use it to get me and my friends wasted.

"What a c-o-o-o-o-l sounding guy," a familiar voice behind me responded with an annoying combination of upbeat salesmanship and unrepentant charisma.

I spun in my chair and saw Pops, the villain in so many of my stories, in all of his annoying glory. Of course, he looked good, an aged version of myself but with less hair, wider shoulders, bigger gut. His eyes still sparkled, though, with a grin that never left his face.

"Been a while, son. Glad to see you back in one piece."

"You're a real ass. You've put me through hell."

"I've made you stronger. That's all."

"Where's Moms or did she finally get around to leaving you?"

"She knows she can't do better. Should be on the floor any minute. We both just woke up for our shifts and she's freshening up in the john."

Nikki placed her hand on my elbow and leaned into me. "It's so good to meet you. I'm Lilian, West's fiancée."

My father elbowed me and snorted. "West? Ha! You've been up to no good."

"I had a good teacher," I said.

"The best. Young lady, my name's Jack and my wife's name is Jackie, a matching pair in a city that loves three of a kind," Pops said, winking at Nikki, his desire to flirt in almost any mixed company unmatched anywhere, anytime, anyplace in the world.

What story could be better than a meeting between a son and his parents with a stowaway girl in tow and four fake names? Four people looking to move on to the next best thing and a little short of finding it. Four liars looking out for number one. The encounter wasn't far off from what I imagined hanging out in a supervillain bar would be like.

"West has told me so much about you," Nikki said.

"I reckon he hasn't even told you the best stories," Pops said.

"Let me start by telling you the Rivet family curse," Pops said, leaning in between us and somehow managing to brush Nikki's breast with his arm. He held up a finger and the bartender slid over a whiskey and soda, the old man's bar drink, a sign that he was well known in the L.

"Jesus, Pops, don't tell this again. I've heard it a million times."

"But I haven't," Nikki said.

Pops sipped his drink like it was a potion and closed his eyes, words tumbling out of him in his best storyteller voice:

"Family legend has it that my ancestor Henri Rivet first came to New Orleans in 1719. He was the captain of a cargo vessel called *Aurore*, which means 'dawn' in French. He had a dream like many in the New World, to sell men to other men. By all accounts, Henri was an innovative businessman. He stacked his slaves spoon style—feet to head, knees to stomach, buttocks to the backs of legs, as a way to maximize the number of people you could store in the holds of the ship.

"The cargo was valuable no matter what state they were in when they arrived. The formula was to give a slave just enough food to make it through the passage from the West Coast of Africa to America. The men were kept shackled at all times, to keep them from escaping, from attacking the crew, many of whom were little more than slaves themselves.

"*Aurore* embarked from Africa with two hundred and eight slaves. Most of them were already sick or injured from their capture and imprisonment. During the voyage, the women and children were occasionally allowed topside to gets some air and exercise. One of the women was a beauty that the captain lusted after to an unnatural degree. Jealous of his crew, he ordered his first mate to haul her up to his cabin and shackle her to his bed. Henri did not know that this woman's husband was already dead, killed rather than be taken captive, and that her son was ill and unable to care for himself. Even if he had known, would it have made a difference to what happened next?

"For forty days and nights, the captain raped the woman, but that's not worst of what happened to her on the voyage. She was allowed outside his cabin once per day, as a reward for her service. She spent the time not staring up at the sun or feeling the wind, but with her head down to the deck of the ship, yelling her son's name and hoping for an answer to come. One day near the end of the voyage, Henri stumbled upon this scene. He knew that he could lose the allegiance of his crew if he was deemed weak. He asked one of his own slave handlers what the woman was yelling about and they told him that she was asking to see her son. He decided to grant the request and that decision changed everything, the course of their lives, and the lives of their descendants.

"It was almost dusk by the time Henri's crew unshackled the son of the slave woman and hauled him up from the bottom hold. So far, the children had been spared the worst of the punishments, the lashings, the rapes. Still, they had no one to look after them and no light reached down to them except for their occasional walks on deck. Even worse, the men who dealt directly with the slaves were from their own tribe, spoke their language, and treated them like cattle. This betrayal of kin was quite possibly worse than any other.

"The boy had a fever and hadn't been able to hold down food. He was like a log cut off from the tree that was his mother, twig feet trembling to hold his weight, hands cupping and blocking the sun poking into the horizon like the end of a fire poker. Fearing a trap, the slave woman did not rush to her son's side. Instead, she said, 'Free my boy or I will make your first-born sons suffer for a hundred generations.'

"Henri laughed when he was given the translation and announced to his crew: 'Here we have a witch from West Africa who has cast a spell upon me. I will show her that I am more powerful than her gods. I will show her the meaning of real power. I will make her son break her heart.'

"Henri looked at the boy struggling to stand and told the slave woman, through her sneering kinsmen, that if her son could stay on his feet until nightfall then he would set both of them free. He waited until his words were translated to mother and son, and the bloody sky bound their curses together into a single curse. The boy was pushed away from the railing and he wobbled across the deck like a drunken dancer. One of the sailors began slapping a rhythm on the bow, and a drumbeat washed over the ship.

"At first, this seemed to give the boy energy and his back straightened, but only long enough to yell one word. It's been said that when Henri's descendants can repeat this word over

the ocean waves then the curse will be lifted. This message
did not get translated as the boy collapsed face first onto the
deck, even as the last light of the day ripped across the cheering
crew. The captain nodded and the boy was tossed over the side,
like a hundred others from that voyage. The boy bobbed and
splashed until the darkness took him.

"The slave woman did not look at her son, but rather at
Henri, mumbling an incantation beneath her breath. That night
the woman was once again tied to the captain's bed as he went
out and celebrated with his crew. What happened next has provided a lot of conjecture among the Rivet men over the years.
Henri raised his glass to the devil and drank down a bottle of
rum, and according to the ship's logs fell dead as a stone. Some
say the moon was red as blood when Henri was thrown over
the sides. Some say the slave woman looked frightened as she
was carried back into the hold.

"The curse, however, was only just beginning. The slave
woman gave birth to a boy on a Louisiana plantation ten moons
later. She had been placed with some of the captain's own kin
and her son was light skinned. The Rivet name stayed with
the sons of the sons of the slave woman for more than two
hundred years. Every Rivet has been a prisoner at some point,
including my father for theft, and his father for murder, and his
father for the murder of a thief. Neither West nor myself will
be free of this curse until we can figure out what that kid said
with his last breath."

I noticed that the revelers on either side of us were quiet;
the old man, a natural storyteller, a conman, had sucked them
in with his tale.

"It's such horseshit," I said, but could hear the tremble in my
voice, and knew that I didn't sound very convincing.

"That was one hell of a story," Nikki said.

"I like this one," he said to me. "Let me see if I can get our
shifts covered and we'll show you both around." Pops slapped
my shoulder and disappeared into the crowd with a few strides.
The crowd swallowed him whole. Nikki smiled at me and I

tried to return it, but all I was thinking was how easy it was for people to walk out of the picture. I felt a panic deep in my gut, fluttering over the drinks and fast food from the highway, spinning inside me like blades of a helicopter waiting for takeoff.

The night with my folks was a blur. They were born entertainers and led us all over the casino—to a surprisingly good buffet, a mediocre acrobat show, and finally a private party in the enormous penthouse suite with a view of the old casinos downtown. They charmed Nikki with their homespun stories of living on a gambling riverboat, and I barely bothered to correct them when truth and fiction became indistinguishable.

I had stopped drinking after leaving the first bar and was nearly sober by the time I got to talk to my folks in private. We sat on lounge chairs on the balcony outside. I had a good view of the magician inside, who hosted the shindig. He went by the handle Presto Cool, and was loud, vivacious, handsome, and swinging Nikki around the dance floor. Moms had lost a few pounds and reminded me of Bianca with her Irish ancestry and all the tools of a party woman: sharp tongue, high cheekbones, auburn hair, green eyes, functional drinker, tomboy, bar maven, pool sharpshooter, big breasts, and a toughness from leaving home at sixteen to join Pops on the road. Her eyes never met mine and kept darting back to the room, making me wonder if a con was on, one way or the other.

"This one is cuter than Deirdre," Moms said in a measured tone, the same one she gave me when she took my arm and blew a kiss near my cheek, no sentimentality or apology for letting me think she'd died.

"And younger," Pops said, smirking.

"And more trouble, too, I'm starting to think."

"That's saying something," Pops said. "Miles told me what went down."

"So, you let your brother know you were alive but not your son?"

"Don't get all dramatic, Buddy," Moms said. "We waited a

year to reach out. You were overseas and then we couldn't track you down."

"Where are you now?" Pops asked.

"In LA, getting myself into a jam while I'm figuring out how to get out of a jam. I was there with Solomon but it looks like he's split on me."

"That boy is cute, but you should know better that to trust his judgment," Moms said.

"You're one to cast stones." It had always bothered me the looks that Solomon gave Moms. Hell, all the boys I grew up with talked about how fine she was—she always ranked first on any MILF list.

"C'mon, tell Pops what's going on. Getting out of jams is our specialty," Moms said.

"You mean getting into the jams that you have to figure out how to get out of?" I muttered.

"Same difference," both of my parents said, and they followed up with "jinx" and a long kiss that made me as uncomfortable as it had all throughout my childhood.

"I'm not here to talk about me," I said. "Or even why the hell you two decided to leave the *real* Louisiana. I want to know exactly what the hell happened to Lucinda."

"Jesus Christ, not again, I can't do this," Moms said, downing her glass of white wine with a practiced tilt of her wrist and neck. She rose unsteadily and made her way inside. She joined Presto and Nikki in the center of the dance floor, gyrating her ass in a manner that no son can look at without thinking about the surface of the sun and permanent blindness.

"Buddy," Pops said. "This is a tough subject for Moms."

"Everything's a tough subject for her. She doesn't like being put under the microscope."

"Who does? She's just trying to protect you. What happened to Lucinda is a tragedy."

"Why the hell don't I remember what happened?"

"It's a defense mechanism. We swept it under the rug, hoping you'd forget about her."

"You can't just do that with everything," I said.

"We were looking out for you, dammit. It turned our family against one another. You've never been the same since..."

"Since what?"

"Since she drowned. Your mother blames herself. For everything. And has been punishing herself for years."

I looked at Moms dancing with a smile that peppered the room like shrapnel, men taking notice even at her age, her hips bouncing between Nikki and Presto. Moms was comfortable in the spotlight but bolted when you tried to get her to open up on any subject at all.

"I think it messed me up too. How can I not even remember my sister?"

"Because she wasn't your sister. The only sibling you ever had was the twin you absorbed in the womb."

"Then who the hell was she?"

"Your Moms had a kid sister Kara, strung out on horse. We looked after her daughter one summer. You took after her like a sister, though. Everyone called her that. Your sister. We had no idea she'd wandered off into the pond..." Pops trailed off in a rare moment of uncertainty, staring out at the night sky, a dark fabric tattooed with signs of something or another.

Tears welled up; the image of Lucinda was suddenly clear. I was the one who found her lying face down next to the dock of the bait shop down the street from our apartment building. I thought at first it was a trick of my eyes, just a trick she was playing to make us worry. Solomon and I had ditched her on purpose earlier in the day. We'd left her behind with the kids milling about in the complex yard, to go out on a run to a gas station to score cigarettes for a habit that we were flirting with having in earnest. It was a game of hide and seek gone awry. We thought she'd stop looking for us and circle back to where Moms was, by the drained swimming pool, drinking mint juleps with the neighbors.

Her face was blue. Solomon's hands shook as he grabbed her from me and sprinted back to the apartment building. I was left staring out at an outboard motor, I was to blame and exile beckoned me, but it would be years before I answered the call and sought penance in the army.

Pops looked at me, "We weren't prepared—"

"To be parents? Yeah, that much is obvious. I'm a mess, Pops. And not in a good way. I thought spending time guarding prisoners would save me."

"Whatever you've done, there are options. There are always options with some creative thinking."

"Is the damn curse even real? Or is it some con to make people feel sorry for us?"

"These things aren't mutually exclusive."

"The hell they aren't, Pops."

"Imagine for a moment that this story was passed down generation to generation. What makes you think each version doesn't change according to the teller? Think of the Bible. Telling stories is the biggest con of all."

"Unbelievable."

"I know. If I had half the talent of Stephen King, I'd own the world."

"I'm sick of the goddamn curse and this goddamn family. Everything's not a joke."

I stood to make my exit and Pops rested his hand on my arm, a calculated movement from a man whose fingers could manipulate cards. "I don't know any other way to get through the bad times. I'm afraid if I don't laugh that I'll never be able to get out of bed."

This was as deep as Pops had ever gotten with me, a moment he ruined with a wink of his left eye, causing me to untangle my arm and turn my back. No, I didn't say goodbye to the old man or Moms either. I just slipped through the bodies on the dance floor, cupped my hand around Nikki's hip, and guided her out the door and out of the L.

It was strange how spending the evening in a facsimile of Louisiana had made me homesick. I was floored by how happy

Nikki seemed after meeting my folks and I was pissed off about how little they seemed to care about my feelings. To them, the incidents surrounding Lucinda's drowning was water under the bridge in a lifetime under the bridge. Christ, I barely even remembered anything about her. And don't even get me started about how they went underground when the hurricane hit. They obviously cared more about getting out of some jam than about my feelings.

Nikki leaned against me at the valet station and I almost tumbled, my sense of direction in the world gone. I slid the bullfrog keychain out of my pocket and tossed them to the valet. The Vegas crowd was older and more male this time of night, not much different from the lineup of perverts trying to get into Club Paradise. A middle-aged geezer with a Chicago Cubs cap mumbled to himself and stared at us with something approaching anger. Was it our age? Or the fact that Nikki was dancing around me like a pole?

Fuck you, I felt like screaming at the jerk behind me, at my parents on the top floor, at everyone and everything around me. Would losing it really be that bad? Maybe it was time to pay for my mistakes. The minivan rattled into the oval entrance, keeping me from doing anything I regretted. I nodded to the valet and tipped a fiver. Nikki slid off me and climbed into the passenger's seat, a look of disappointment on her face. She didn't want to go home but was kind enough not to break my balls about it. Nikki could sense I was done: with chitchat, with our little adventure, with trying to explain why we were taking off so quickly. The strip was less depressing at night. There were fewer kids being pulled around from place to place. The darkness hid the cheesiness and desperation that lurked there. I obeyed the traffic signs and pulled onto the highway, cruising just under the speed limit.

"What can I do for you?" Nikki asked.

"Read to me," I said, gesturing to the book on the dash.

I was nearing the end of the last book in the Travis Mc-Gee series. Nikki picked up *The Lonely Silver Rain* and opened the glove compartment where a bare bulb leaked just enough light. She found my place in the novel, crumpled my book-mark receipt, and jumped into the action. Her voice was steady as she read to me about the inevitable fight with the bad guy, where Travis got hurt and the villain got what he deserved. That wasn't the end of the novel, though. There was more to the story. A door opening instead of closing. The detective's daughter appeared at the end, angry and looking to lash out. In the end, though, they found closure, and it looked like he had something to live for. I found myself getting choked up and rubbed my fist in my eyes so I wouldn't cry.

"Anything wrong?" Nikki asked.

"That was the last book. I need to find a new author," I said. "Damn pain in the ass."

We didn't talk the rest of the drive home...could I even call LA home? Traffic was light on the highway after midnight, and we made good time. My head churned with emotions that I had a hard time identifying. My relationship with my parents was still unresolved. I was not willing to give them the bene-fit of the doubt. I thought about Travis McGee and how he always seemed to get the short end of the stick, but also went to the wall for the people who were important to him. Here I was looking for role models in books of made-up people and made-up stories. Not sure what that said about me. I only knew that there were people close to me that I could help: Solomon, Alice, Nikki, even myself if I could get my shit together.

Highway 10 took me along a river of tweakers, partiers, and early morning exercise buffs to land at Club Paradise a hair before five a.m. I eased down the brick driveway into the back lot and for once, there weren't any other cars in the driveway ex-cept for an old red Mazda. All the drunks and the dancers had made it back home, all except one. The moments just before sunrise were truly the quietest at the club, especially now that the filming was complete.

"Pull over," Nikki said, and I humored her, cruising to a spot next to the garage door where the liquor and food trucks unloaded, where I first saw her brother Iman. Wordlessly, she took my hand and we headed for the back service entrance. She took a set of keys from her purse and let herself inside. I wondered if Big Z knew that she had a set. We didn't turn on any lights, instead navigating by the exit signs and the track lights in the rafters. Nikki led me to Big Z's office and held a finger to her lips at the door.

"This is stupid," I whispered.

"No, it's crazy smart. Like a fox," Nikki answered, strutting into the room like she owned it and everything else in Club Paradise. She flicked on a lamp and stopped next to a framed picture on the wall of Big Z in his younger days in a wrestling pose. Niki carefully placed both arms around the Plexiglas and lowered it to the floor. A safe was inset in the wall behind it. Nikki grinned impishly and moved the tumblers like a practiced pro. The lock clicked open.

"The combination is my mom's measurements…when she met my dad. He never lets her forget that she *used* to be hot."

"I'm supposed to be security here," I protested.

"Then you should notice just how easy it is for someone to come in and steal one hundred grand."

With a flip of her wrist, she held the door open, and I saw an impressive stack of bills next to a closed briefcase. She closed the safe, spun the dial, and hung the photograph back on the hook covering the money. I noticed a pill bottle on Big Z's desk next to an enormous black mug that the owner carried around the club to hide whatever he was drinking. I held up the plastic container and read the label: *Rohypnol*. There were roofies in Big Z's office. The closed door behind his desk led to a staircase up to an apartment suite where he would often spend the night with one of the dancers. My thoughts churned. Was Big Z a rapist? Was Solomon providing him the drugs? What exactly was I supposed to do? Nikki snatched the bottle out of my hand. Recognition and then disgust washed over her face.

"Maybe there's an explanation for this," I said.

"Yes, there is," she said. "This isn't going to end well."

18

SHADOWS OF THE SILVER SCREEN

The next morning, I dropped Nikki off at the garage entrance and hoped no one saw me. I felt like a new man after the ride home, tired though I was. The shadows around me could not keep up. I pulled the minivan into the back lot of the apartment building I now called home. I was in an ass-kicking mood. Because it's difficult to kick your own ass, I figured I'd start with my friends. First stop was at Alice's. The early morning sky was blue for once. I wondered if it had sprinkled yesterday, an intermittent occurrence that cleared the smog for a day or so. I used my key to let myself in. Blake cupped his forehead at the dining room table, eating some generic Cheerios knockoff, perusing the ingredients on the box as though they held the secrets to eternal life. He mumbled through his fingers, "Going to quit drinking one of these days."

"Today could be one of those days," I said, circling around him to the kitchen.

I poured myself half a cup of coffee in a chipped mug, filled the other half with non-fat milk, and gulped it down. I rinsed out the cup, returned it to the dish drainer, and headed over to Alice's room. The door was cracked open and I could hear her on her cell phone. Not normally one to eavesdrop, I found myself edging closer to her room, craning my head.

"Zelda, my friend beat him nearly half to death and he still won't stop calling." There was a long pause.

I pushed the door open. Alice lay on the bed, phone to ear, in her underwear. She smiled at me weakly, not bothering to cover herself up. I dangled her car keys in one hand and held my hand out for the phone with the other. She sighed and we exchanged items.

"Zelda, this is West," I said into the phone. "I'm going to have to ask you to stop talking to Alice."

"That's fine. I'm talking to you now. Alice's son has moved on but I have a spirit from your past that wants to talk to you. A light. A little light who's worried about you."

The origin of Lucinda's name was light. That much I knew. I didn't believe in psychics, yet I couldn't hang up. "I'm lost. I'm not sure where to go."

"You're running away from yourself," Zelda said. "No one's that fast."

"You're a con woman. Zelda's not your real name. Leave me alone."

"You're fooling yourself. West isn't your real name. You're in danger. You need to save yourself."

My hands shook and my voice cracked, but I found some resolve. "I'll save myself. From paying you money."

I hung up on Zelda and sighed.

"She's good, isn't she?" Alice asked.

"Zelda's an ass. I know her type. Stop listening to her and listen to yourself. Do you want your husband back in your life?"

"I can't go back."

"That's something I understand." I sat on the edge of her bed, pausing until she looked away from the window and we made eye contact.

"I hurt everyone around me. First, my son. Then, the girls in the club. I help them fill out their job applications and set them up with that monster Big Z."

"You didn't make him into a monster. That's on him," I said.

"I'm an awful person."

"No, you're not. You're lonely. You're afraid. You're grieving for big things and small things. It's no way to live. Trust me."

"You really messed Greg up," Alice said. "He's afraid of me."

"That's a start." Not knowing what else to say, I kissed Alice on the forehead and rose from the bed.

I slipped out to the living room, closing the door behind

me. Blake, as though sensing what I'd done or, more likely, eavesdropping, took my place in the room and closed the door. The coffee had not made the slightest dent in my tiredness. I plopped down on the couch and put my phone in the charger with my ringer on in case I was called in to work. The voices in the next room continued, sometimes louder, sometimes barely audible. I curled up and was swallowed by sleep as deep and dark as the Mississippi River.

Nothing was what it seemed to be. Not even in my imagination. I woke from a dream where I had the superpower of floating. Even there I had limitations, only able to hover over the ocean. I was trying to get somewhere in LA, but I couldn't make my way onto land for fear of crashing. There was a buzzing sound in my ear warning me of losing altitude and I woke to Bianca's text: *You need to go to Paradise to cover Deacon.* I didn't mind the occasional bar shifts. It gave me something to do instead of pining for Nikki (yes, she was really starting to get under my skin) or worrying about Solomon. Nikki had also sent me over a dozen texts but I wasn't in the mood to answer her. Our journey to see my folks seemed less cathartic in daylight, and I wondered what, if anything, I had accomplished. I slipped into the bathroom to wash up in the sink and change clothes. No time for a shower.

I headed out the door to work, feeling not quite real, insubstantial in every way. It wasn't just the lack of sleep or real food. It was more—a lack of connection to the world around me. The roots that kept me from falling over were now loosened. My folks, Deirdre, now Solomon. I inched slowly along the carpeted second-floor apartment walkway. There were discarded cigarette butts outside Solomon's door. I looked around in all directions, trying to be nonchalant about my paranoia of being watched. I tiptoed to the half-opened bathroom window. Ambient music floated from inside to wrestle with the whooshes of the freeway overpass. Had Solomon come back? I circled around to the front door and let myself in with my key. The apartment was almost unrecognizable, the victim of what looked like a week-long party. Drug paraphernalia was scattered on the coffee table next to a pile of discarded clothes, all of it wet and smelling like bong water. Pizza boxes, fast-food bags, and empty beer and wine bottles created a Tetris-like effect on the floor.

I found Solomon in his bedroom, or at least I thought I had, until I raised the covers and found the mannequin lying in bed. Had he really just disappeared without saying goodbye? Without his clothes? His DJ gear? His car? I searched the apartment for clues and nothing seemed out of the ordinary, except in the kitchen. It wasn't just that the dishes were cleaned and put away. There was a single word on the fridge spelled in letter magnets: *DANGA*. That was expression we'd used as kids for danger. It was a warning we gave ourselves when we were pushing the limits and should probably run for cover. In this case, it was meant for me. It made me feel better, somehow. It was just like Solomon to trick people in believing he was around by making his place look like it was being lived in. Did he owe people money? Did he piss off the wrong Pourali for sticking his penis or his nose where it didn't belong? There were way too many unanswered questions for my liking. Common sense told me it was time to get out of town but not until I was certain that Solomon was safe, that Nikki was safe, that Alice was safe from her ex-husband and herself.

It was going to be one of those days. I could feel it the moment I walked over to Club Paradise and noticed that someone had applied lipstick on all the statues in the front garden. I subbed in at the door for Deacon who had a casting call in Beverly Hills to audition for the role of a college wrestler. He was already dressed for the part, decked out in a tight-fitting Lycra one-piece and headgear. He roared when he saw me and gave me a thunderous high five, tagging me into my shift. It looked like he was prepared to go the extra mile to try to win the role.

"Gotta stay positive," Deacon told me before racing out the door.

Everyone at Club Paradise seemed to be wearing disguises, including the dancers who always played the part. There were new auditions today, and one of the strippers caught my eye—a young woman with incredible legs and light brown skin, dressed in a full ballerina outfit and an eerie white mask that covered everything but her lips. The DJ who had replaced Solomon was be-bopping with triangle sunglasses and rhinestones glittering on his sheer white shirt. The dude looked baked and was gathering song requests from the half-dozen applicants next to the main stage. Usually, Alice mama-beared the newbies through the process but she was home sleeping in, leaving the girls with even less protection than usual.

Flynn, known for being wound tight, was extra agitated when he stormed inside for his shift. "If anyone asks to see me, send him back to the bar and hang back a step or two in case things get out of hand," he said.

"Anything I should know about?" I asked.

"It's just business." He reached into his pocket and pulled out a postcard for his horror film *Sirens*, premiering that Saturday night at a Beverly Hills venue. "Can you work the door for this event?"

"If I clear it with Bianca."

"She's going to the event too. Shouldn't be a problem. They're closing down the place early. First time in years."

I didn't know what concerned me more—that Flynn had worked there that long or that they stayed open on Christmas and other holidays. Normally, I tried not to watch the dancers, out of respect, but I kept an eye on the auditions, waiting for the ballerina's turn. The first few women weren't up to snuff, even though one of them was athletic enough to spin on the pole before wiping out. A few onlookers snickered and I moved over to help the dancer up before she waved me off. Just then a man strolled through the main entrance; he had no eyes for the dancers. He was all business. The guy was about my height with thinning dirt-blond hair, wrinkles in the corners of green eyes, and a face that I recognized from my time in Kabul. He'd been one of the freelance interrogators during my first deployment. This was messed up. Why would I run across the same man in two different hellholes halfway across the globe? Either the universe was trying to tell me that I couldn't run away from the military or that I was going insane.

I thought I saw a flash of recognition before the stranger made a beeline toward the bar. I followed several paces behind and readied myself. Flynn exchanged a few terse words that I couldn't quite catch and he instantly brandished the bat. The guy didn't seem scared. Names were exchanged and they began talking about a friend of Flynn's, George Stark, who'd funded the independent film. After that, I lost track of the conversation as the replacement DJ cranked up the music for the next dancer, the hot ballerina with the mask. Not sure why, but I was mesmerized. The ballerina knew what she was doing. She shimmied and spun, and the movement tickled the back of my brain and reminded me of my dream of floating.

The interrogator stepped back from the bar and had a quick exchange with the DJ before sliding by me. The dancing ballerina did a scissor kick onto the pole and the interrogator whispered to me, "Take care of yourself, Buddy." How could he have possibly remembered my name? Or was it just another coincidence? I thought about following the guy outside, but Big Z emerged from his office through the women's dressing room and ogled the new dancer.

Time stretched for an eternity, until the ballerina dismounted the stage and sidled up next to me. "This is what you get for avoiding my texts," Nikki whispered from behind the mask.

"Jesus," I said to everyone and no one as Big Z nodded toward me, then the girl. Without Alice here, was I the one supposed to pimp out a daughter to her father?

"So, are you ready to take off with me?" Nikki purred in my ear, nuzzling my neck. "Cat got your tongue?"

I pulled away like I'd gotten a jolt of electricity. I needed to

do something before Big Z made his way across the room. It
was time for me to do what I did best. I grabbed Nikki's arm
and pinned it behind her back, propelling her toward the door.

"Hey!" she complained loudly for show and then hissed
under her breath, "So you like to play rough?"

I steered her past the ticket booth and out into the sunlight,
our shadows blurring together on the doorjamb.

"I'm cleaning out the safe and taking off Monday," Nikki
said calmly. "Five in the morning. The place will be dead. You
better be here to give me a ride."

"Or what?"

"Daddy will blame you no matter what you do. You might as
well enjoy his money and his daughter."

I thought I heard footsteps and shoved Nikki toward the
sculpture garden. "And don't come back!" I barked loudly,
shouldering my way back inside through the curtains.

I found myself staring at Big Z's chest, his bulk filling almost
the entire doorway. I fought the urge to hurt him where all men
are weak: in the kneecaps, in the nut sack, in the eyes. Instead,
I slapped both hands together like I'd just taken out the trash.

"I was looking forward to giving that one a foot rub, if you
know what I mean," Big Z said.

I felt sick to my stomach. "She was underage. Her father
would be really pissed if he knew."

"That's a shame," Big Z said. "She had a lot of potential."

"Don't we all," I said.

Big Z roared with laughter and slapped me on the back
before striding back inside. Likely, he'd be looking for new victims among the remaining auditions. This creep needed to be
stopped from preying on down-and-out women. My head was
spinning. Too much was happening too quickly. After seeing
the interrogator, I wondered if the universe was telling me that
perhaps I should deal with my AWOL status and return to face
my punishment. The universe was also telling me that I should
take off with a young girl, barely legal, after stealing her father's
money in an adventure destined for an epic blow-up.

Everyone was gossiping about why Solomon had vanished. The most popular theory being he was holed up with some woman, partying like mad. Flynn called him a *flake*, unlike me, and it barely made a dent in the conversations among the regulars, now obsessing about the release of the film, filled with jitters and praise for their latest work. One night, Judd made me pose while he etched my likeness in his notebook. When he was done, he showed it to us, and everyone claimed he was drunk. I knew better. He had a gift. The figure in the charcoal sketch was me, but not me. All the lines were blurred, every part of me in motion, as I stood at the end of the bar.

Blake became my partner in crime for looking after Alice, both at the nightclub and back at the apartment. She was drinking heavily, something I hadn't seen her do before. We had a plan to keep her sober for the premiere and removed all the beer and hard liquor from the apartment. We even asked Flynn to keep an eye on her to make sure she didn't pull a bottle from the bar. Iman was our eyes on the outside. We thought we had every angle covered. That didn't stop her though from gobbling a few valiums she'd gotten from one of the dancers the night of the premiere. Blake paced in his suit, trying to put enough coffee into her to sober up. Meanwhile, I was just trying to find enough clothes to put together a formal outfit.

I ended up back in the wreckage of Solomon's apartment to borrow some threads. I never had much of an opinion about clothes one way or another. In some ways, wearing a uniform like I had in the army or as a security guard at Club Paradise comforted me. The less choices the better. I went through the options in his closet. Solomon was thinner than me and it took me a while to find something that would fit and wasn't too hipster-ish.

I took my phone out of my pocket. I texted Nikki, asking her advice on what to wear. She made me send her photos and weighed in on each one. The burgundy jacket was too much like that of a pimp. The tan coat was professorial. Finally, we settled on a plain black suit coat, twenty years out of fashion, probably something that Solomon purchased in some thrift store on his trek across the American Southwest.

I pocketed the phone and slid the jacket over my usual black T-shirt. It was too late for me to rewind the clock and act like some kid texting with his girlfriend. I craved this normalcy, but the stakes were already too high. Lord knows what would happen if Big Z searched my phone. I wasn't sure what any of the Pouralis were capable of—they all seemed desperate in their own ways. I needed to escape, unharmed, like Solomon had done (or at least I hoped so). And would that be with Nikki and the money from the safe, or on my own?

Deacon was supposed to chauffeur the family over to the movie premiere but volunteered to drop me off beforehand at the theater in Beverly Hills used occasionally for award shows and premieres. I don't think his audition had gone well. He was also still prickly about not being in the film and didn't plan to see it. He dropped me off at the entrance and hightailed it out of there. My arrival caught the attention of a passing Beverly Hills police cruiser. I took my hands out of my pockets and smiled at the car. The cruiser inched by to the end of the block, then sped up, flashing its lights and blaring its siren. A man in a red coat held open the door at the theater entrance.

"Where's your invitation?" the doorman asked.

"I'm an usher."

"That makes more sense," he said sarcastically. "That jacket is a treasure."

It looked as though I was woefully underdressed. Wouldn't be the first time. I saw the regulars decked out in formal attire lounging in the catered lobby and made my way over to a small group surrounding Flynn. I was also the last of the four ushers to arrive, but I'm pretty sure I didn't need the speech on how to treat the guests. I knew I was there in case someone got blasted and nasty on free wine and needed to be eighty-sixed.

As the first guests started to line up outside, Flynn veered over to me—it was clear he'd already taken advantage of the complimentary wine bar.

"Alice is the star of my movie, and do you know where she is?" Flynn asked.

"I'm giving her some privacy right now," I said.

"But you know something?"

"Same as you. Her ex has been harassing her."

"Dammit."

"You okay?" I asked, leaning over and providing him with an arm.

"Of course, I'm not okay. I'm screwed if I can't get distribution."

"Maybe you have more time than you think. Your friend may surprise you."

"Like your friend Solomon surprised you by taking off and leaving you holding the bag. Kid, everyone here wants a piece of you for one reason or another. You'll pay for whatever your friend did and whatever you're planning on doing."

I stationed myself in the corner so I could watch the room and the stairs leading up to the screening. Flynn paced the floor, chatting with everyone except for the regulars who dominated the line for appetizers. The bartender/screenwriter looked more stressed than I'd ever seen him. I kept an eye out for the man who'd financed his film or for anyone who might be threatening him, but there was nothing out of the ordinary. That is until the Pourali family appeared at the front entrance. Deacon held the door open for them and it made me wonder whether I'd lost my standing as their private security guard or if my relationship with Solomon was souring my employment. When I started working for the family, I told Big Z that one of the conditions was that Solomon needed to work there as well. Things were coming to a head. My departure was imminent. The only question was whether I wanted to throw my lot in with Nikki or slip away to destinations unknown.

Big Z, in an all-black suit and black tie, led Bianca in by the elbow. Both mother and daughter were dressed in gowns, with Nikki's low-cut blue dress leaving little to the imagination. My heart caught in my throat. Nikki glanced at me knowingly before looking away. Beautiful women, in all cultures and backgrounds, knew this look. It said *I'm unavailable* which made you desire them even more. Deacon led the threesome to the VIP section while Malik, in a tux, made a beeline to the front of the wine bar, jostling the first man in line and shouldering his way in. If looks could kill then Malik would have been a dead man. Meanwhile, Iman circled over to me and pulled an envelope out of his back pocket.

"It's payday, you fool," Iman said. "Buy yourself some new threads. You look homeless."

"I kind of am," I said. "How are all your girlfriends?"

"Glad they're no longer dating you, for starters."

"Don't tell me you're kissing your sister," I said, then immediately regretted it.

"Jesus, you're an idiot. I don't care what the hell you're doing with sis but my dad and Malik do. Pull yourself together, fool."

"Don't listen to me. It was a bad joke."

"You still haven't figured out how to lie. I warned you about this. My family is filled with bullshitters. Every single one of us can twist you up. Me included. You are not LA material, son."

"Maybe not."

"Relax," Iman said, cracking a smile. "I've got your back, bro."

The kid jetted over to his brother and snatched one of the wine glasses from his hand, downing it in a practiced swig. Malik shrugged and pilfered a bottle of red wine from the station, following his brother toward their seats up front.

What the hell was my problem? I wasn't long for this town, but I shouldn't have let Iman know I was involved with his sister. Idiot. I needed to get my head out of my ass.

I waited until the lights fell in the theater before snagging a seat in the back row. I was too lost in thought to completely track what was going on in the film. On screen, Alice had a near-death experience and her shadow had been collected by the grim reaper. A piece of her soul became the siren—it hounded her movements and tried to summon all the people who'd wronged her to an early grave. Alice was fighting her alter ego at first, even though some deserved death. Then the siren became less discerning. A simple argument could lead the siren to convince her loved ones to travel into harm's way.

I wasn't much of a critic, but it was clear that Alice was, by far, the best performer. She didn't care about being an ac-tor and maybe that's why she was a perfect monster. In some ways, she'd become like her film alter ego the past few days, a ghost version of her former self. Two parts of her—present and past—trying to reassemble. The film was spookier than I wanted to admit, and I jumped when a hand grabbed my arm. It was Bianca. She leaned into me so that I felt her breast pressed against my shoulder.

"I almost hit you," I said in a low voice.

"That's something I'm used to," Bianca whispered, rolling up her sleeve to show me a purple welt. "That's why I need protection. Take a look at this and tell me if it will do the job."

She plunged her hand into her purse and passed me a hand-gun, handle first. I snatched the weapon from her, horrified. I looked around but all eyes were focused on the screen. I checked to make sure the safety was on, holding the grip gingerly.

"You need to get rid of this," I said, placing the pistol back into her bag. "It's more likely that you're going to kill yourself or your kids than Big Z."

"He's not leaving me a lot of choice," she said, sniffling and rubbing her face and makeup against my shoulder.

"You always have a choice."

"Divorce isn't an option with some men. Not when he threatens to track you down, no matter where in the world you hide. He's bankrupted us with this horror show of a club. He and his brother bought up a block of businesses that don't pay the bills. He's crooked to the core. I know it. And my kids are suffering."

"Kids are always suffering. A lawyer is a better option than a gun," I said.

"I thought you were a soldier," Bianca whispered like I'd betrayed her. "I thought you'd understand."

"I do understand," I said, but I was addressing air as Bianca headed back to the front of the theater.

I turned back to the movie and watched Alice, dressed as the siren, hold a balloon on a string and whisper in the ear of a professor who'd groped her earlier in the film. She let the string go and it drifted out over the edge of a parking garage. The professor smiled and stepped toward the balloon, reaching out for it. His momentum carried him over the railing and he disappeared. There wasn't a sound. Not until screams rose from the street below and a distant siren wailed.

19

SHADOW DECEPTION

I woke to Alice's husband Greg leaning over me with a stained green couch pillow in his hands. I shot up, adrenaline pumping, and rolled off the couch. I hooked one leg behind his ankle and readied myself with the other to break his leg. What was he thinking—that he could smother me like an invalid or small child?

"Don't," Greg said. "It isn't what you think."

"I think you're on the verge of needing a cane for the rest of your life," I replied.

The traffic from the street below mewled like a cat, a constant thrum, white noise to passersby. Time seemed to have no meaning. It could be daybreak or mid-day. The light poked through the shades tentatively, like a child unwilling to be born.

"I'm a broken man," Greg cried out and fell onto the couch. He rolled over and curled up in a ball, and I noticed that his dress shirt was stained with blood. His scent was pungent, like the POWs at the former Soviet air base. I got to my feet and cocked a fist. I heard a noise and then someone appeared and rushed at me. I saw the siren. I blinked and the image became Alice, still dressed in her gown from the premiere, her makeup smeared on her face. She touched my back in a sisterly way, and then kneeled over her husband. In the bedroom, I could hear snoring and figured Blake was sleeping off the bottles of wine he'd polished at the open bar.

"Sweetheart, I can't take this any longer. You need to come home with me," Greg said.

She held his hand. "You need to leave."

"I hate it here. The trash on the street. The noises in my head. I've lost my faith in God," Greg said.

"I'm not sure I ever had it."

"We'll die alone."

"We were dying together," Alice murmured, her fingers caressing her husband's bruised cheek.

I felt awash in something I could barely fathom. Her chipped black nail polish intersected with the mottled skin from the pummeling I gave him. Everything in the world was steeped in phantoms, every path filled with emotional landmines. I could be like Don Quixote and swing my fists at the world, or I could choose a way to help the people who mattered. I had no compass now for my decisions. Not even big-hearted detective Travis McGee could help me now. I barely noticed the swirl of activity around me. Moments passed. Perhaps minutes. Perhaps eternity. I turned to the door in time to see Greg and Alice walk through it.

Alice turned back and tossed me her frog key ring. "West, I'm going to take Greg back home. Go ahead and use my van if you want."

"Are you coming back?"

"Alice in Winterland can do anything because she's magical," she said. "It's why I invented her."

"I invented West, too. Buddy is the name of a guy who drowned years ago. I can't seem to shock his heart back into beating."

"He'll be okay. Eventually. Please tell Blake what happened. Tell him I love him. Tell him that he didn't do anything wrong."

Just like that, Alice was gone and the walls felt like they were closing in. I thought about waking Blake, but our commiserating would have to wait. I got a text from Bianca ordering me to come and get the family at the country club tennis courts. Nikki had been strangely quiet after giving me her directive to run away with her. She'd said her piece; the ball was now in my court. What would I do if she tried to run away from home? I wasn't sure. Maybe seeing her again would help me figure out my next step.

When I got to the garage, one of the town cars was missing. Deacon must have dropped off the family. I was feeling superstitious, like I was a beacon for all things bad. I felt the invisible eyes of the law on me during my drive over. I kept expecting the other shoe to drop, for someone to run my name through some database and then pull me into a holding cell. But the glazed-over security officer of the Oakwood Country Club waved me through.

I found the Pouralis in the packed stands at the main tennis court. Iman was playing against a boy who was a head taller, blond, and grunting with each of his shots. Not that it mattered. Iman's reflexes were impressive to watch. He was a dervish on the court, making improbable saves on rocket volleys, returning them with topspin. I took one of the few empty seats and noticed Nikki sitting with her parents and Malik center court. Big Z was pumping his fists in an animated fashion, and Bianca gripped a glass of wine like the earth was tilted and it was the only thing keeping her from being pulled away.

I lost myself in the match, the two opponents trading shots and points. In the final set, Iman slowly lost ground, losing a step, yielding to the power game of his opponent. He sweated profusely and had given it everything he had until it was match point. On the third match point Iman was late getting to the baseline and he yelled in frustration, unable to turn on the ball, launching the shot into the stands. Whether by aim or circumstance, the ball landed straight between his parents' seats. Bianca yelped and tossed her wine onto Big Z, leaving the wrestler red-faced. Iman looked up at his parents, his anger melting, before turning away.

Nikki's eyes met mine and I released my own fist. I could feel my nails drawing blood in my palm. I tried to smile at her but she looked away.

The ride back home was silent. No one spoke. When I parked inside the garage and opened the back door, Nikki winked at me before joining her parents. Iman trailed behind, launching his tennis racket into a plastic bucket and disappearing inside the steel door. Malik closed the door behind his brother and looked me over from head to toe.

"Can I help you with something?" I asked.

"For your sake I hope so. I just wanted you to know that I hold you accountable for Solomon's actions, just like I hold him accountable for yours."

"Don't sound like a fucking fortune cookie," I said.

"Don't think we're pals just because we're the same age. That's a mistake your friend made," Malik said, running his fingers through his slicked-back hair. "I'm the boss around here. I say jump and you say I'm already in the air."

"So, what exactly am I supposed to do?"

"Let's imagine your friend Solomon owed me something but decided to skip town instead. That would make you the next up to do the right thing. You wouldn't want to do the wrong thing, trust me."

"I don't trust you though," I said, hoping to keep the conversation going long enough to verify if Solomon had left on his own.

"Maybe you're too smart for your own good," Malik said, clicking the garage door opener.

I hesitated for a moment and Malik waved bye-bye to me, a sneer on his face. I wanted to smack it off him like I'd popped Lasicky. Then I thought about what I had to lose. *Walk away* I told myself, turning and strolling outside.

"Pussy," Malik said just before the door closed.

"Lame way to try to get the last word," I muttered, not sure if Malik heard me, and realized my statement could very well apply to myself.

The Flapjack Shack was a haven of sorts. I hid out here when I could no longer stand being at the club and I didn't want to be alone. After my interaction with Malik, my guard was up, and I felt encumbered like the gear we wore on the road transporting prisoners from place to place. Afterward, you hurried to pull off the layers, but there was always another item to be removed. It was time for me to extricate myself from the Pouralis, from my misguided commitment to protect them. There were too many layers, though, to jettison at once.

I pushed a forkful of pancake around a pool of syrup, staring into the brown smear.

"I didn't peg you for having a sweet tooth," Bianca said, approaching the table and taking a seat across from me. "You shouldn't eat stuff like that as an adult."

"Maybe I'm not an adult."

"Good lord I hope you are if you're fucking my daughter."

"Jesus, you and Nikki have two things in common. You both are stalking me and swear like sailors."

"Sailors? I always pegged you as more of an army man."

"So did you have the apartments bugged too?"

"That Blake has a mouth on him," Bianca said. "You can't just trust anyone to keep your secrets. I think you're different, though, Buddy."

"Why is that?"

"You've already proven that you can keep your relationship with my daughter under wraps."

"Maybe I did that for self-preservation."

"For me, it doesn't matter why. Only that you'll do what I say."

"Do you think that little of me?"

"No, I think that much of you. Tell me you'll fuck me."

"Okay, Bianca, I'll fuck you," I said sadly. "But not in any way that will satisfy you. I'm no good at relationships. I'm not a person. I'm a ghost."

"That's why you need women like me and Nikki in your life," she said, flagging down the busboy and handing him my half-eaten plate. "In the end, we'll give you a reason to be a man."

Not knowing what to do with myself, I headed back to the bar of Club Paradise to get drunk. None of the regulars were there except for Blake, matching every drink of mine with three of his own in his own attempt to get hammered.

"They have a hangover," Blake explained when I asked him where the other bar flies were. "A movie hangover. Happens every time we finish one."

"This one's different," Flynn muttered, listening in to our conversation. "It has to be. I can't last another year here."

"My liver can't last another year here," Blake slurred.

"You should go home," I told Blake, but he shook his head and patted me on the shoulder.

"It's the one place that reminds me of Alice."

"Me too. But she's not coming back. You know that? She left with Greg."

"Never say never," Blake said and laughed at his own joke.

Flynn poured a glass of water for the ex-NSA agent after that and I barely listened to his litany of complaints with the world. I'd been keeping an eye out for Big Z.

I grew restless after I poured Blake into a cab and found myself doing a security sweep, first of the defiled statues in front of the shuttered windows and then out back to check the cars. No one was out back giving or receiving sexual favors or smoking dope. Sunday nights tended to be quiet, with some men choosing to spend time with family, firing up the barbecue or watching sports on the TVs at home. I continued down the back alley that ran alongside the Far Horizon warehouse, trying to get enough distance from the building so that I might be able to see a star or two. The lights were out in the warehouse and the fenced entrance was closed but not padlocked. I opened the swinging gate, moving it slowly so that it wouldn't creak.

There weren't any cars in the back lot. Yar and his associates were home with family, too, perhaps. The battered green garbage bin was propped open by too much junk and a familiar item glinted from the light of my phone. It was Solomon's first guitar, the orange Gibson, alongside his other guitars. His records. His recording equipment. This situation had moved beyond the Pouralis being pissed at Solomon. They were now trying to erase him from their establishments. There had already been no paper trail, no employment documents. Now there would be no traces, no fingerprints, nothing to show that he'd ever supported the family's legal and not-so-legal activities. What the hell had happened to my friend? I found a large cardboard box in the bin and started loading it with Solomon's possessions.

My phone was almost out of juice as I waited for the digital clock on it to inch toward five o'clock. It had been hours since I'd climbed into the back of the minivan with a box of Solomon's possessions. I stretched out on the back seat, staring out the window at the far tower. Light leaked through the closed blinds in Nikki's bedroom, so it was difficult to tell if she'd been awake all night. Slipping away with a woman I'd been sneaking around with felt illicit, but I also felt the urge to protect her, to find a way to a better place.

The idea of the money was like sugar. It sweetened the deal of our running away but in the end would prove to be like the pie that Solomon and I had taken on our rafting trip. It would not last. Money never does. The sweetness would fade away and harsh realities would bring me back to all my problems, all the ways I was wasting away. Our future, even fueled by money, was a mirage. It was childish to think that someone as young and lost as Nikki could help me find a life where I did not hate myself and everyone around me.

The smart move was to take off now in the minivan and leave Nikki and her family to their own fates. I thought about all the boxes in my life. The ones in tree houses, hiding away from childhood. The prison in the mountains of Kabul. The coffins for those falling under bombs. The smaller boxes for children drowning underwater. The club was a trap, too. Nothing escaped, not even light. I feared what would happen to me if I returned, but I knew I wouldn't be able to live with myself if I didn't.

20

SUNRISE SHADOWS

There's something about the belly of sky just before sunrise. It ripples slowly, a cocoon working toward bursting open. The sky and I were as one as I checked the time on my phone and slid the door of the minivan open. There had been no movement in the parking lot for hours. With no afterparty tonight and no film being shot in the funky basement, it was quiet. Because we were so far from residential areas, there were no dogs barking. Just the faraway whooshing of automobiles, the ballad of Los Angeles, the motion of going nowhere and thinking you're going somewhere. The creature on the frog key ring stared up at me while I turned the tumblers in the lock and slipped inside the unlit club.

I stopped in the hallway to let my eyes adjust and I noticed one light had been left on in the building. The door to Big Z's office was cracked open and a sliver of light projected onto the wall next to the women's locker room.

Each step I took lasted forever. Every natural instinct I had told me to head the other way. I couldn't leave, though. Not without seeing Nikki. Not without looking her in the eyes. I pushed open the door and she was there all right. But she wasn't alone. Nikki moved from the open safe behind me and shut the door, placing a hand on my shoulder. Bianca leaned back against the desk in a pink tracksuit with two curious additions: leather driving gloves and a handgun pointing at a figure in the office chair beside her. Big Z was out like a light, duct-taped to the chair, a bottle of prescription roofies opened on the desk next to him. Mona, dressed in a black cocktail dress, sat in a chair next to her sister-in-law. The Pourali women were all waiting for me. It was a trap. In a flash, a voice called out in the back of my head *you're fucked* even as my brain tried to push the pieces of the puzzle together.

Bianca flicked her phone and I heard my voice emanate from the tinny speaker, "Ok, Bianca, I'll fuck you."

"You asshole," Nikki said. "Men are pigs. You're all the same."

"Nikki, I was set up. You have to believe that."

"Did you really think my daughter would ever end up with someone like you?" Bianca asked, her usual sarcastic lilt in full effect. "You were just a means to an end."

"The end of a life?" I asked. "Count me out of whatever weird-ass shit is going down. I'm walking out now before you do something stupid. No one will ever know I was here."

"Not true," Bianca said dismissively.

"At first, we thought Solomon might be the man for the job. But you're the one. I'm sure of it," Mona said. "Big Z has fucked all of us. Literally. And fucked us over."

"It's time he gets what's coming to him," Nikki said, her hand caressing my shoulder.

I stepped to the side to gain some room and I almost bumped into Big Z. His face looked peaceful—not like that of a monster. "If you are victims how can you live with making a victim out of me?"

"You'll get the money," Nikki said, pointing to the open safe. "You're already on the run."

"I'm bailing. You have other options."

"No, we don't," Bianca said. "And your fingerprints are already on the gun."

That stopped me in my tracks. Of course. Bianca had set me up at the movie theater

"So, you're in on this?" I asked Nikki.

"You have no idea what it's like to live with a beast like my father."

Bianca smiled and kicked Big Z in the groin. He didn't move, dead to the world.

"It was bad enough what he did to us. But all these girls in the club were forced to do unspeakable things," Mona said. "He fucked me any chance he got and dared me to tell my husband."

"Go to the cops. You have witnesses," I said.

"Witnesses like you. Fucking unreliable witnesses who will bolt before any case goes to court."

"That's not…" I started to mouth the words *not true*, but I stopped myself from lying. "Bianca, why don't you just leave with your kids? Get as far away from him as you can?"

"I already told you that he'll track us down and kill us. Maybe not Iman. But me and Nikki for sure," Bianca said.

"Is that what you want?" Nikki asked, running a fingernail along my cheek.

"Stop playing me," I said. "What the hell do you expect me to do about any of this?"

"For you to show us that you're a good person. I'm going to put a bullet in his head and leave the gun behind. You're going to take the money in the safe and head for the border."

"You think I'm just going to let you frame me?"

"Plan B is that I shoot you and then tell a teary-eyed story for the cops about how I caught you red-handed with the money from the safe after you blew away my husband." Bianca pointed the gun directly at my head. "I had to protect myself and my daughter. I had to shoot the bad man."

"You think my life is worth this little?" I asked.

"My private investigator sure thinks so. You're already a wanted man. You're headed for jail one way or another. I'm giving you freedom."

"Nikki, talk her out of this. We can go to Berlin. All of us together. Like you planned."

"My German class was a ruse. You're just cute enough to fuck but get one thing perfectly clear—I don't give a damn about you."

Nikki walked over to her mother and yanked the gun from her hand. "I'm sick of this."

She pointed the weapon at her father and her hand shook. She grabbed a stained pillow off the couch and pressed it against Big Z's head with her left hand. The barrel pressed into the fabric. This was my chance to race out the door, to try to clear myself of this family, to run from the curse that had hunted me my whole life. But I couldn't. I walked over to Nikki and placed my hand over her fist, steadying her hand. The dead zone in my palm covered her knuckles. Both of our prints were on the gun. Both of us were desperate.

"You're not alone, Nikki. No one should have to face things alone."

An explosion filled my hand with something approximating love. It was beyond my control, beyond our control. My ears rang and I closed my eyes. This was good. Finally. Peace. No shadows here in the dark.

First light was starting to break as I navigated the minivan along the almost empty city streets. There was something freeing about sailing unimpeded through the normal daytime gridlock. I whipped northward on Veteran Avenue alongside the graves of soldier who fell in WW2 and veered westward along Sunset Boulevard. The road narrowed to two lanes winding along tree-lined streets that led up into the hills, past a Buddhist self-re-alization center, no cars or people to be seen, the end of the world glimmering at sunrise. Before I knew it, I had made my way to where Sunset dead-ended into Highway 1 and a stretch of beach next to a closed restaurant.

I sat at that intersection for what seemed like forever. No cars coming up from behind. No cars passing into or out of the city. Too early even for surfers to hit the beach. On either side of me was a gas station. In other cities this was overkill, but it made sense at the beginning or end of the road. You needed to make sure you had options.

I tried not to think about how another woman had played with my emotions—the only things Deirdre and Nikki had in common were me and a strong need to change their own lives. I didn't value myself enough to demand what I'd needed in a relationship. This was true for my lovers, parents, and friends. I couldn't blame anyone but myself for the mess I was in. Even though I'd been threatened, I still felt guilty for the desperation in Bianca's eye, in Mona's words, in Nikki's actions. They were in deep shit but that didn't absolve them. Just like I shouldn't be absolved from my decisions.

The light finally turned and I crossed the highway, pulling into a nearly empty parking lot. The coolness of the morning air enveloped me as I emerged from my minivan embryo. My face was damp and I ran my fingers along my cheek. Finally, another traveler appeared behind me and pulled into one of the gas stations. I breathed in the briny air and propelled myself toward the ocean. I'd spent months in LA on the west side of town and this was my first visit to the Pacific. My own fault. I kicked off my shoes and socks and made my way to the surf. The coldness of the water licked at the bottom of my feet.

I gripped the smartphone that Bianca had given me and marveled at how those devices, built to make us less lonely, only caused us to misunderstand each other. The device buzzed in my hand; someone was trying to reach me. It could be the women in Club Paradise. Or not. Solomon reaching out from the road. Or the great beyond. Nikki pinging me from the passenger's seat of the van, money between her legs. Or not. My parents apologizing. As if. Or none of these things. Perhaps it was Malik, looking for an explanation about why his father was asleep…had disappeared…or was dead I could not be sure what had happened. I could not keep the facts straight. Perhaps my dead twin knew. Perhaps Lucinda. Perhaps Alice on the other side of the looking glass.

None of us were any different from cavemen clutching torches, keeping the shadows at bay. We carried those tiny lights with us everywhere and all they did was blind us. I cocked back my arm to toss my phone into the ocean, but it would be a useless gesture. It wouldn't change who I was or what I had or hadn't done.

The question of who the real monster was settled over me. Bad people did bad things. Formerly good people could become bad people. People you trusted betrayed you, and a life without trust is no different from a battlefield. I'd always daydreamed that I was a hero, but it was a vision based on grief, on my inability to keep people safe, including myself.

What was next? In front of me was an impossible chasm as large as the history of a nation with nowhere left to hide. I could feel the rays of the rising sun behind me, and I tried to envision the word that could lift an ever-migrating curse. It was simple enough to imagine. It would be like believing in something as big as God or the vastness of untapped potential. To the right and left were the borders of two separate countries calling with the promise of more years undercover, drifting in the wake of people and places, an ongoing quest to be lost.

"Light," I said, and wondered if that was the word that would free me from the curse. My shadow splayed out before me, a line that I no longer wished to follow.

My parents lay behind me in Las Vegas, experts in the ways of difficult passages. They would be able to help me sort out whether Solomon was still alive and if I was free from the trap that those desperate women had set for me. They would find out if Big Z was okay and hide me until I was able to face my own mistakes. They would check the facts and contemplate the odds. They would be there for me. They would take me back to the beginning of the story, before I drowned in myself.

I turned around to face the dance of a new day.